Flight to Terror

Flight to Terror

Dayle Courtney

Illustrated by
John Ham

 STANDARD PUBLISHING
Cincinnati, Ohio   2713

Thorne Twins Adventure Books

Library of Congress Cataloging in Publication Data

Courtney, Dayle
  Flight to terror.

  (Thorne Twins adventure ; 1)
  Summary: Alison and Eric draw upon their Christian teachings to overcome the many problems they encounter when their airplane is shot down by African terrorists over the Valley of Death.
  [1. Terrorism—Fiction. 2. Survival—Fiction. 3. Christian life—Fiction. 4. Twins—Fiction] I. Ham, John. II. Title. III. Series: Courtney, Dayle. Thorne Twins adventure books ; 1.
  PZ7.C83185F1   [Fic]   81-5632
  ISBN O-87239-468-9   AACR2

Contents

1 • African Sky Terrorist

The edge of dawn colored the eastern sky.

Long hours had passed since takeoff from London's Heathrow Airport on the night flight to Capetown, South Africa. The lean, athletic sixteen-year-old American in aisle seat 23B was feeling edgy.

Eric Thorne had walked the aisles of the 747 until he felt he could describe every passenger. He had even tried unsuccessfully to start a conversation with the cute brunette on the aisle seat next to the galley. His excuse was that he wanted to be nearby in case any food was being handed out. But no success on either score—very little conversation, and even less food.

A baby's cry came from the aft section. Eric adjusted his seat for the hundredth time and decided to relax. Most of the passengers were dozing. Twin-sister Alison on his right was unusually quiet.

How strange, Eric thought, for her to be awake and not talking. It gave him an uneasy feeling.

Perhaps his edginess was due, he decided, to the unsmiling blonde across the aisle who eyed his every move. It was clear that she had no intention of starting a conversation. Eric first noticed her when she had boarded the plane and was struggling to stow her carry-on luggage of two large camera cases. He felt sure she was an American. A reporter perhaps.

Maybe she recognized him from U.S. newspaper pictures taken during Inauguration Day festivities with Gram and Gramps. It was still hard to remember that Gramps was now Vice President E. Bradford Thorne.

Having a grandfather who was Vice President of the United States did have its drawbacks though, like having to keep a low profile on this trip. The instructions from the Secret Service agent in London had been clear.

"Forget you have any connection with the V.P.!" he had said cautiously just before Eric and Alison boarded the plane. "Remember, kids," he had warned them, "you are just two Americans traveling to visit your father in South Africa. And he's there to do a project for the International Agricultural Foundation. Now, don't you forget it. Good-bye. And keep out of trouble!"

Dad cared little for the Washington limelight. He was glad to be away on this foreign assignment and happy at the prospect that the twins would be with him for their summer vacation months.

There was one thing Gramps and Dad did agree on. They insisted on Eric and Alison having as normal a life as possible. Secret Service people who came and went were carefully handpicked. Most of the time they melted into the scenery and didn't even identify them-selves. One of them could be on this trip, Eric sup-posed. On second thought, he doubted it.

As the aircraft sped southward five miles above the African desert, Eric settled his athletic 5'11" frame into a comfortable position and turned toward the window. In seconds he became conscious of a black spot growing larger in the early morning sky. He would have sworn that spot had not been there a moment ago.

Eric blinked his eyes to rid himself of the annoying optic. It was strange how that spot on the Plexiglass was growing. Ridiculous.

Alison stirred with sudden tension. "Eric, look!" she said, pointing to the growing black object.

Maybe he should tell her it was only a flying saucer, Eric thought. She actually believed in those things.

By this time he realized that the window speck was making him jittery. He looked around. Others were be-coming aware of the fast approaching object. The pitch of voices in the cabin increased sharply. Members of the crew were suddenly heading forward as though summoned by some urgent command.

One more glance out of the window and Eric knew that the black spot had become a black plane. It was closing fast on the airspace of their commercial 747 jet. Clearly the black silhouette was arrowing toward them.

"Eric! That plane's headed straight for us! What fool would play chicken five miles high? The pilot's crazy!"

Other passengers were watching it now. People on the other side of the plane left their seats to get a

9

better look. Curiosity quickly turned to alarm. The black plane's unwavering course was too purposeful, too deliberate. Its collision course with the 747 seemed intentional.

"It's trying to hit us!" someone shouted.

"If he does, he goes with us," Eric responded hotly.

The mystery plane had already broken one international law by invading the airspace of the 747. And few passengers doubted that the pilot had something more diabolical in mind.

"He's going to hit us!"

"We're going to crash!"

The voices exploded in many different languages.

Eric grabbed Alison's hand. His sense of time seemed to expand for a split second. Suddenly he realized how dear his twenty-minute-older twin was to him. He wondered if they would be sharing their exit from life as well as their entrance.

"Why doesn't our pilot do something?" a male voice in front of them barked with anger.

Before the question was completed, their pilot did.

The 747 dipped sharply as the alien plane thundered above and beyond it. Passengers were thrown forward against their seat belts by the force of the pilot's sudden tactic.

"Sorry," the Captain's tense voice came on the plane's loudspeaker. "No time for a warning." All the public relations juices that had flowed freely in his voice in earlier announcements had drained out.

"Place all hand luggage under your seats. Fasten your seat belts. Flight crew, take your seats," the Captain's voice clicked off.

10

"We're being attacked!" Alison cried out. "Who—?"

"Maybe we've violated somebody's airspace. They change the rules every other day in these parts of the world," Eric quipped nervously.

"Who would be crazy enough to attack a British commercial jet?"

"Here it comes again!"

Eric's eyes followed Alison's pointing finger. The insanity was not over. Now the black, unmarked plane was high above the 747 on the left again. It turned slowly, a mere pinpoint in the sky. Then it was diving. Its shadow expanded like some great black bird of prey.

Alison pressed her knuckles to her face. "Eric—!"

He squeezed her hand more tightly. The plane was speeding toward them once more.

"We're a terrorist target!" the graying African in the row behind them spoke in an audible gasp. In the unbelieving, frozen silence his words echoed with terrible truth.

The frightened passengers were jabbering hysterically in a dozen languages. Behind them Eric and Alison heard a woman's voice praying.

"Belts tight!" the Captain ordered as the speaker came to life again. "We're turning."

The plane shifted abruptly, falling to the right in a maneuver for which the big transport was never designed. Alison was thrown against Eric, but she continued to stare through the window. "It's still coming. It's still coming! It's shooting at us!"

The metallic thunder of bullets ripping into the forward part of the 747 drowned all other sound. Screams filled the cabin, now a shambles of food trays, magazines, and personal belongings. The African woman hugged her two small boys to her.

"It struck the pilot's compartment!" Eric yelled, moving to unfasten his seat belt in the urge to go forward and see what damage had been done. At that moment he was thrown back against his seat as the giant plane pulled itself up from its sharp descent.

"Thank God! Someone's at the controls," he breathed.

The stark terror diminished a little as the plane leveled out. Glazed eyes searched the heavens for the mysterious black plane, then followed its course as it passed under the airliner and speared into the sky on the other side. At the top of its mile-high loop it turned once more and began a second death dive.

"Eric! This can't be happening to us!" Alison moaned.

Enraged and helpless, Eric put his arm around his sister's shoulders. Together they watched the black plane plunging toward them and saw a narrow streak of fire burst from its wing.

"Here comes a rocket!" someone shouted.

It was true. A missile of death flamed toward the 747. The jet pilot banked desperately to the right, but the rocket swerved too, following the heat of the left outboard engine.

Perhaps the maneuver did it. The missile grazed the engine instead of striking it directly. An explosive blast and a ball of flame erupted beneath the wing. The stricken engine trailed fire and black smoke through the sky.

Plunging heavily to the left, the crippled airliner spun toward the desert far below. Outside on the starboard wing the flames of the disabled engine died under a shower of automatic flame suppressor. Only black smoke continued to flare like a comet's tail against the brown sea of sand that was spinning toward them.

"If he can just pull up that wing," Eric said. "If he's just got enough flap on the other side—" His fists clenched as if he were trying to right the plane with his own physical energy.

The landscape slowed its spinning, and the cabin floor leveled as the pilot gained control once more. Energy expended, the passengers gradually became quieter, watching the swiftly rising desert with deathly fascination.

"What if that plane comes back?" whispered Alison. After its last attack the anonymous black plane seemed to have vanished in the vast, cloudless sky.

"Its pilot may think his last shot finished us off," answered her twin.

"Well, didn't it?" Alison's voice was tight and tinged with bitter, helpless anger as she struggled to hold back her fear.

Eric's chest and stomach pained from the tension that gripped him.

"There's a one-in-a-million chance our pilot can land this plane with one engine out, and who knows what else—"

The speaker rattled once more, the Captain's voice strained almost beyond recognition.

"Captain McGuire speaking. We have been attacked by an unknown aircraft. Our radar indicates it has retreated now. We've lost contact with control at Nairobi as a result of our damage. At present we have partial control of our aircraft. Our ability to maintain level flight and flying speed is very critical.

"We are now over the Valley of the Great Rift. It gives us a fair chance of making a safe landing. The plateaus on both sides of the Rift are covered with too much growth to allow us to attempt a landing there.

"Keep your seat belts tight. Use the oxygen masks if you need them. We are approaching the floor of the Rift for our landing. Bend forward, with your head down. And pray for our safe landing. That's all."

The speaker shut off. The babble of voices and cries rose again as the passengers caught sight of the forbidding landscape below them.

Outside on the tip of the splintered wing, pieces of metal fluttered in the airstream, sending heavy vibrations through the 747. Partly torn from its mount, the damaged engine shook violently.

"That could tear the whole wing off!" Eric shuddered. Clinging together, the Thorne twins watched with glazed eyes.

Some of the passengers were moaning, crying with a helpless fear and waiting for the bizarre, hideous drama to end. In spite of the pilot's efforts, the airliner slewed and twisted as it slid down the sky. The damaged wing hung low like that of a stricken bird.

Alison shook her head as if to rid herself of thoughts hammering through her mind.

"Eric, do you think we'll make it?"

"Who knows? Probably not even the Captain knows if we'll make it!" Eric's voice reflected his fear.

15

From a seat behind them a woman's voice spoke gently through the space between the backrests. "There is One who knows," she said. Her voice was as comforting as what she was saying.

"It's up to God now. Whatever He allows will be all right."

Alison reached for her hand and held it a moment. "You're right," she said. "I'm just so scared it's hard to remember that."

"Right!" Eric answered, fighting the sickening fear that struggled to overcome him.

The gentle, firm voice with a faintly English accent began to pray.

"Our Father which art in Heaven—"

Eric and Alison joined in with tight, almost unrecognizable voices. There was a giant sob as the dignified black man hunched over, head on his lap. Within seconds he recovered enough to join in.

"Forgive us our trespasses—"

The "Amen" of the prayer was lost in a thunderous impact. The banging and rattling of the crippled engine erupted in a shriek of tearing metal. The useless engine tore loose, crashed once against the surface of the wing, and fell free.

Suddenly the only sound was the vibration of the loosened wing panels as the plane slid and crabbed its way out of the sky.

Eric and Alison watched as the sandy floor of the Great Rift came into clear view. Streaked with white soda deposits, the sand lay in uneven waves. A few green patches of struggling scrub growth were all that broke the desolation.

16

The ship was fast losing altitude. It was down now to the level of the plateaus on either side of the valley.

Eric guessed that they were about two thousand feet above the valley floor. The perpendicular walls were about thirty miles apart. Between them lay one of the most desolate landscapes on the face of the earth, the Great Rift.

As the plane sank below the tops of the cliffs, someone in the forward part of the cabin began to sing hysterically, a piercing, painful sound. Another cried and moaned in a language Eric did not know. A harsh voice commanded them to shut up. But the crying and singing continued.

"The Captain will have to make a belly landing," Eric said. "The wheels could never roll in that sand," he added, surprised by the matter-of-fact tone of his own voice.

The landscape blurred now as it rushed past the window. Only a few more seconds—

"Now!" a voice from the speaker commanded, "heads down!"

Eric and Alison bent low, the seat belts tight about their waists. They could see the little boys and their mother doing the same.

"I love you, Eric," Alison said in a hoarse whisper.

Eric turned to look into her velvet brown eyes. He thought fleetingly of the times he wished he'd never had a twin sister—and had told her so. Or the many times he wished she'd get lost. But that was all past.

"I love you, too, Twinny" he answered tenderly.

Metal screamed against sand and rocks as the belly of the plane scraped the desert floor. The ship thundered against the earth and bounced into the air, hanging an instant as if suspended. Then it plunged and smashed the earth again.

Eric felt as though his ribs had broken against the restraint of the seat belt as he was flung from side to side. Alison moaned out in pain as the lurching threw her head severely against the side of the cabin. Others screamed from sudden, sharp injuries.

But the ship's momentum was not yet spent. It twisted and slid sidewise. It dipped to the right, and the wing tip gouged the sand. Then, as if the plane were some living monster, the tail whipped in the opposite direction and the fuselage cracked in two.

Abruptly, it was still. The shriek and clash of metal was gone. Finally the only sound was human—the cries of hurt and terrified people.

2 • Emergency Landing

Eric snapped open his seat belt the moment the plane stopped screeching and sliding. His ribs were aching, his nose was bleeding, but no bones seemed to be broken. He turned to Alison, who was holding her side where the seat belt had bruised her. Still belted, she reached for him, laughing and crying in hysterical relief.

"We're safe, Eric. Thank God, we're safe!"

He stood up and jerked the lever of the emergency door, which faced their seats, and threw the panel outward. It was a ten-foot drop to the ground.

A white-faced steward appeared and called out the emergency exit instructions. The move to the exit began an orderly response to his "Don't crowd, please." Then suddenly somebody yelled, "Fire!" A new danger had erupted.

Eric jerked Alison's arm and unsnapped her belt.

"Quick! We'll be crushed in our seats!"

Mobilized by the new fear, Alison scrambled to the edge of the opening. Eric held her hands and steadied her.

"Remember all that physical fitness, Sis. Now. Drop!"

She let go and dropped downward, the first person to hit the valley floor.

Before Eric could get his balance for his own leap, a violent shove plummeted him through the hatch. He flew into the air and fell sprawling, narrowly missing his twin. Another body thudded to the sand almost on top of him. He felt a hard leather case brush his shoulder. It was the wiry body of the black man who had been seated in the row behind him. There was another body. And another—

With extreme effort, Eric detached himself from the falling bodies and gave Alison a vigorous shove.

"Get out of the way—quick!"

They scrambled a few yards on hands and knees, then stood and ran to a safe distance. Over their shoulders they saw a stream of panic-crazed human beings tumbling and screaming through the small hatch, hindering their own safety as they were forced brutally through the exit. There were broken glasses and injured arms and legs for many as they smashed to the desert floor.

"They'll kill each other," Alison cried helplessly. "Panic is so pointless." In helpless amazement she watched the swinging fists and bloodied faces.

What about that English lady, Alison wondered—the one who had prayed with them as the plane descended.

"Have you seen any of the people who were sitting

near us, Eric? I wonder what's happened to them?''

Eric pointed to the window behind the emergency exit. "That lady—she's just sitting there, waiting for the pushing and shoving to clear. She's got enough sense to keep cool.''

The smell of hydraulic fluid was strong and unmistakable. It hung like a blanket in the hot, dry air. So far no fire had broken out.

The tall African man who had sat behind them appeared to have twisted an ankle in the fall. They watched him now limping toward the jagged opening in the fuselage just behind the wing. The rear section was bent toward the port wing, the tail still thrust upward against the sky.

Framed in this opening, dazed, injured passengers now appeared and began to drop to the ground. Thankfully it was just a few feet away. These passengers had suffered most from the crash. They had been thrown about in wild confusion as their seats tore loose from the floor mountings. Those who had been hurled against jagged edges of torn metal were bleeding badly.

The danger of fire seemed to be past.

Eric and Alison approached the gaping hole in the fuselage just as a man staggered out and headed off like a sleepwalker into the desert.

"Follow him, Alison, and bring him back. Try to get those who are able to walk into the shade under the wing," Eric told his twin. "I'll go inside and see if I can help.''

Alison ran after the man wandering aimlessly under the blazing African sun and gently guided him back to the plane. In the nose of the plane, a door was being forced open. The faces of anguished crew members were visible through the glass.

Eric climbed inside the battered fuselage. It was like a scene of war. Bleeding, unconscious human beings were sprawled about like dolls that had been tossed aside by a careless child. One or two were stirring and trying to get to their feet. In spite of their own injuries, two stewards were already at work helping the passengers. Eric took a cue from them and began to help clear the area by assisting the least injured passengers to the jagged opening and down the short descent to the ground.

At one point he found himself in an emergency briefing. The Captain was holding paper towels to a bleeding gash on the right side of his head as he instructed his copilot and the flight engineer.

"That's right, keep moving the wounded to the shelter under the wing. Tell everyone there is no danger of fire. We dumped the fuel."

He turned to his flight engineer who was standing beside Eric. "Patterson, this young man will help you with the most badly hurt. Round up as many able-bodied passengers as you can get to assist. Collect all the blankets and pillows to make them as comfortable as possible."

He turned to his copilot. "Thomas, break out all our first-aid supplies. Check the passenger and cargo manifest and report anything you find to me. See if there is a doctor aboard. Get some volunteers to help the girls keep a sharp eye on the galley—or what's left of it."

The copilot nodded and moved away to take care of

those tasks. Eric saw that he was in pain. The young man had torn off part of his shirt to try to stop the bleeding from his hand.

The Captain turned to the task of assessing the human damage. He seemed eager to talk to each survivor personally. Eric caught up with him when he stopped for a moment to wipe the stinging sand particles from his face as a gust of hot wind swirled by.

"Captain, do you know who that black ship belonged to?"

He shook his head. "Nothing. We know absolutely nothing. Our radio was shot out with the first blast. I'm afraid we live in a world where terrorist acts can happen without reason and without warning."

There was another question Eric had to ask. "Sir, could some particular passenger have been the target?"

"Entirely possible, but we have no evidence."

The Captain turned to his dreadful task. Eric remembered seeing him as they had boarded the plane in London, a big, jovial Irishman in his late fifties. His red hair was just beginning to gray. He had been joking then with some of the stewards. Now with the smile gone and his face lined with anguish he looked ten years older. His shoulders slumped as he walked away.

Eric went to help a stewardess and one of the passengers lower four lightweight stretchers from the aft section of the plane that had begun to look like a great broken toy in a giant sandbox. The tall, distinguished-looking black man who had been seated behind Alison was already busy.

He introduced himself.

"I am Doctor Ngambu. May I have a look?"

Eric recognized the medical bag as the one the Doctor had carried off the plane. He bent to examine the unconscious man Patterson and Eric were about to load on a stretcher. A large, heavy man, he had collapsed in his seat. His lips were blue.

Dr. Ngambu nodded. "I will administer a stimulant. Then he can be moved."

Quickly he prepared a hypodermic and made an injection. The man began stirring as he was being placed onto the stretcher.

Under the Captain's direction, Dr. Ngambu took charge of the cabin crew, three stewards, and two stewardesses, all of whom had some training in first aid. His earlier seatmate, the woman who had prayed aloud with them, came forward now and offered help. She introduced herself as Mary Hastings, "Forty years a missionary and nurse in Africa." Dr. Ngambu responded to her introduction with respect.

"Ah, I too am a believer, Miss Hastings," he said with a genuine smile.

Other passengers quickly volunteered or were enlisted. Dr. Ngambu and Miss Hastings worked feverishly, attending the most seriously injured and the dying. Alison was assigned to help those who could walk. She herded them into the shade of the wing, where most of them sat on the hot sand, dazed and shocked in disbelief.

The first task of the emergency team was to stop the bleeding of those who had been torn by jagged metal and glass. Improvised tourniquets and bandages were applied. Help for the more seriously injured in need of immediate surgery was unavailable. Dr. Ngambu did what he could, sewing serious wounds, applying makeshift splints and supports where possible. Internal injuries he could do nothing about.

Quickly, quietly, efficiently, the Doctor directed his assistants with little more than a nod of his head or a glance of his eye. Eric was fascinated by his obvious skill. He watched, wondering where this man came from.

When the rear of the cabin was finally cleared, seventeen bodies remained. Captain McGuire ordered them left there, to be removed and placed in shallow graves when the sun had gone down.

"Please let me watch over my brother's body!" a bereaved woman cried. The Captain assured her that all the bodies would be recovered when the rescue teams came so they could be returned home for formal burial. Mary Hastings gently led her away.

Eric and Alison moved about to comfort the sorrowing and the wounded. At Miss Hastings' instruction, they used few words and the best kinds of communication for such hours—tenderness and caring. A sip of water. A search in the cabin for a few comforting possessions. Listening.

The stories were heartbreaking.

The man and woman from Glasgow who refused to be separated had saved all their lives for this trip. Now, neither of them would live to see tomorrow's sun come up over the escarpment. A Capetown man was returning after twenty years to marry a childhood sweetheart. There were few complaints. A great pride in these brave strangers lumped in Eric's throat.

Wearily, he and Mr. Patterson laid the last stretcher

case on the sand and beckoned one of the medical team to look after him. Nearby lay a man they had not brought out.

"He must have made his own way and collapsed there," the engineer whispered to Eric.

The man was an elderly man, probably in his late seventies. A shock of bushy white hair contrasted with the sun-bronzed skin of his face, gnarled by time and the elements. He was making no sound, but his face twisted and his body writhed in uncontrolled pain. Blood saturated his shirt and trousers. Eric wondered how he could have made his own way out of the plane in his terribly injured condition. He was a tough one.

Captain McGuire was looking at him, too. He knelt and opened the man's bloody shirt. A wide gash held a pool of blood that drained down his side as the man twisted in pain.

"See if Dr. Ngambu can come," the Captain said to Eric. "This man needs help quickly."

The injured man raised his head and glared. "No!" he exlaimed with as much strength as he could muster. "Not him! Not that nigger doctor! Just wrap a bandage around me, and I'll be all right."

"A bandage won't stop that bleeding. You've got to have more than that."

"No!" The man's head shook violently. "Jakob Vroorman will never be touched by any nigger doctor."

The Captain's face hardened as if to say, "Then bleed to death if that's the way you want it!" The eyes of Jakob Vroorman closed as his head sagged weakly.

"Watch him," the Captain said to Eric. "I'll speak to Dr. Ngambu."

26

Eric nodded. The man was obviously an old Afrikaner, probably descended from the original Boers who settled and farmed the veldt of South Africa. And he was one who would deny the equality of a black man to his dying day—a time that was not far off unless Dr. Ngambu could help him.

In a moment the Captain returned with the Doctor, who was now limping and appeared near exhaustion.

"He's in bad shape," said Captain McGuire, "But he won't be grateful for your help. He's an old-time, hard-bitten Afrikaner, who won't give a black man the right to breathe the same air. Perhaps others should have greater priority."

Dr. Ngambu smiled faintly. "I do not practice my profession for gratitude. I can probably help him if there are no internal injuries. The wound can be sutured. Please ask Miss Hastings to come assist me."

Eric hurried to Mary Hastings and explained what was going on. Her brown denim skirt and safari blouse were stained with the blood of those she had already helped. They reached Jakob Vroorman's side just as he was opening his eyes again. He got one look at Dr. Ngambu bending over him and uttered a snarl, then he turned his head away to avoid looking at the man who was working to save his life.

Mary Hastings shook her head and brushed her graying, short-cropped hair back from her forehead.

"You say this man's name is Jakob Vroorman? I knew I had seen him before," she said. "I met Jakob Vroorman when my father first took me to South Africa. He was impossible then and he hasn't improved with age."

27

Dr. Ngambu set to work with the meager facilities available. Eric moved away in search of Alison. It must have been two hours since he had seen her. He found her on the other side of the broken fuselage, sitting on the ground with a young French couple who looked scarcely older than teenagers themselves. The girl was holding a baby that looked to be less than a year old. The top of its head was hidden with bandages. Both the parents had been crying. Alison had been crying, too.

Alison introduced Eric to the young couple. "This is Michelle and Laurence Duchene. This is my brother, Eric."

They nodded solemnly and answered in a combination of English and French.

Michelle was dark, with long, black hair to her shoulders. A petite, beautiful girl, she seemed tiny beside Laurence, who was tall and large-boned.

"Their little girl, Marie, was hurt in the crash," Alison said. "Dr. Ngambu says she has a skull fracture that needs to be operated on, but he can do nothing without hospital facilities. I've been praying with Michelle and Laurence that help will come in time."

"I'm sorry about your little girl's injury," Eric said. "The Captain expects it will be only a matter of a few hours at most before we are located and rescue ships are sent here."

"Laurence had an offer of a good job with an engineering company in Cape Town," Michelle said. "We thought starting out in some new place would be wonderful—and now it's hurt our little girl."

Her words were spiritless, like a recorded announcement.

28

Of all the passengers aboard the plane this little French family seemed the most pitiful to Alison. She wanted to lift them up and tell them their plans weren't a mistake. That it was not their fault that their baby had been injured. But all she could do was watch and stay by them.

"Do you need water?" Eric asked. "I'll see if I can find some for you." He wished he could assure them that help was only hours away. But he was not so sure himself that they would all be found soon enough.

"Alison brought us water," Michelle said. *"Merci."*

Eric walked back to the other side of the plane. He scanned the cloudless sky. It was nearly four hours since the attack. The plane was now three hours overdue at Nairobi, and they had been directly on course. A search should have been started a long time ago.

Alison came up beside him and shaded her eyes to scan the brittle blue sky.

"I've been watching all afternoon, Eric, and I haven't seen or heard a single plane overhead. It would be awful to have to spend the night in this deserted place. I heard Dr. Ngambu say some of the injured would not survive the night without surgery." Eric had given up expecting rescue until the next day, but he didn't have the heart to tell her. He had also begun to wonder if Nairobi had helicopters suitable for the job. No planes of any kind could land on the rough desert floor. Turning, he rested his eyes on the green plateau of the escarpment.

"A fellow called Lars says that those vertical cliffs are about two thousand feet high. If only we could have landed up there we could have had some shade and cooler air. There would have been plenty of water, and even animals for food. If we stay here long enough to need that, of course,'' he added quickly.

In the furnace heat and with the shortage of supplies, Eric asked himself how they could survive even forty-eight hours. But surely they would be rescued long before then. They had to be. There was no reason not to think otherwise.

Cries of fright and pain from the injured had diminished now, but there was still an undercurrent of moans from those Dr. Ngambu could not quiet with drugs.

Eric turned back to give a hand to the stewards who were inventorying the scant food supply.

''What's the food situation?'' he asked.

''We have food prepared for two meals,'' the English steward answered. ''But it will soon spoil in this heat. We will divide it into one-third servings, to be given out sparingly. Just in case—''

The afternoon sun dipped early below the western escarpment. The wreckage of the plane was close to the east side of the Valley, in the last streamers of sunlight. The shadows of the distant cliffs crept over the huddled band of hurt and desperate people, then slowly climbed the steep eastern wall.

Scant servings of food were doled out by the plane's crew. Water was limited to a quarter of a cup except for the severely injured who could not eat. The oppressive heat lessened a little as shadows covered the Valley. A faint current of air stirred.

In the last rays of twilight Captain McGuire stood and asked for the passengers' attention. The side of his face was drawn with pain from the injury to his head.

"I want to thank you for the wonderful cooperation and courage you have shown," he said. He paused as one of the stewardesses repeated his words in French.

"We have no information about the attack on our plane or who was responsible. It appears to be another of those insane terrorist actions plaguing the world."

At this point a woman jumped to her feet and shook her hand in anger at the Captain. The woman wore a tailored skirt and blouse with a tie still knotted at her neck in spite of the heat. Her long blonde hair swung like a mane as she moved. Eric remembered her well. She was the dour blonde who had watched his every move on the plane. Now she was the one who complained about everything. She even blamed the crew for the disaster.

"It is criminal negligence!" she shouted at Captain McGuire. "The Government should provide military convoys for commercial airliners in this area. Your company is utterly irresponsible for flying unprotected aircraft through savage territory!"

"And who are you, Madame?" asked the Captain.

"I am Sarah Lander of the World News Service."

"I suggest that as soon as you get back home, Miss Lander," said the Captain, "you write the president of our airline and express your views."

"I shall do more than that! I shall publish to the whole world the story of the stupidity that threatens the lives of air passengers."

"In the meantime, please lend a hand to our survival. In other words, we would welcome you as part of the solution instead of the problem.

"Searches will be made for us," the Captain continued. "I felt quite certain we would see search planes today. Evidently problems have been encountered that prevented their reaching us this soon. We should expect help to arrive by tomorrow at the latest. They will probably drop food, water, and medical supplies to tide us over until helicopters can get us all out.

"Until then, we will have to be very careful in our use of what we have. I am sure we can count on you all to continue your courageous consideration of one another. We will attend to the needs of the injured as best we can. Try to make yourselves as comfortable as possible for the night. Some of you may wish to make beds for yourselves on the seats inside the aircraft. Thank you."

From somewhere on top of the plateau the blood-curdling scream of an animal punctuated the night.

3 • *Valley of Death*

As darkness began to fall and the air rapidly cooled, some of the men built a fire with driftwood gathered from the desert floor. Soon a ragged circle was formed around it as the more sociable moved their blankets together.

Strains of Lawrence Welk's music floated out from a cheap tape recorder, and someone tried to encourage a sing-along, but the response was unspirited. With the darkness came sounds of birds and animals on the escarpment above. Expressions of discontent from a group of still-angry passengers continued to erupt now and then.

Eric's offer to help in the temporary burial of the dead was kindly but firmly refused by the crew. He and Alison huddled together on the outer rim of the circle about the fire.

"Funny, I haven't seen Captain McGuire for about an hour," Eric mused.

Not more than ten minutes later a hand-held torch flared in the darkness beyond the tail of the 747. Here and there persons separated themselves from the group of lounging and sleeping passengers.

"Why are all those people moving toward that torch light!" Alison queried.

Eric jumped as he felt a hand on his shoulder. "You and your sister are asked to join us," an Irish voice said very softly. Eric turned expecting to see Captain McGuire. He saw instead a large man in a colorful native shirt wearing a French beret tilted over one side of his face. The unusual outfit was completed by tinted sun goggles. Alison grew uneasy.

"I have been informed that you are Eric and Alison Thorne, grandchildren of the Honorable E. Bradford Thorne, Vice President of the United States," the Irish voice continued. "We were advised you were on board."

A sudden flash of light from the campfire revealed that the features were indeed the Captain's. Glimpsing the concern on Eric's face, Captain McGuire apologized for the temporary fright his disguise may have caused. It was, he assured them, in the common interest. He moved off in the direction of the torch, which was already reduced to a faintly glowing ember, and nodded for them to follow.

"Please excuse this attempt at secrecy," Captain McGuire began abruptly and without ceremony when they reached the meeting place. The only light now was from the desert moon. As far as Eric could tell there were about twenty persons in the group. Easily recognizable were Dr. Ngambu and Mary Hastings.

34

"I have asked you to join me here for several reasons, not the least being your helpfulness and cool-headed response in the hours since the crash. You know I am greatly concerned that we saw no sign of search planes today. I expected that when Nairobi lost radio contact with us and we became overdue, an immediate alert would be issued.

"Something is terribly wrong, and I have not yet discovered what it is.

"Because we must work from the possibility that no such help will come tomorrow either—" There was a sharp gasp from his listeners. "—I feel it is necessary to increase the number of people whom I can count on to give help to the suffering and to infiltrate the camp with as much hope and strength as possible until help arrives."

Eric was surprised to see that only two crew members were among the group. Patterson, the flight engineer and Thomas, the copilot, both in off-duty clothes. The Captain was taking no risks.

"The only possible explanation for this tragedy is that we were the target of a terrorist attack. Our passenger list includes three persons with a link to the top level of government in their countries."

Again there was a stir of interest in the company. Eric and Alison moved closer in the darkness.

The Captain continued. "I am withholding the identities of these persons in the interest of their safety. I don't want these individuals to become the target of the negative faction. When I speak to the group in the morning, I shall not mention their presence. I shall attempt to divert their attention by pointing out how thankful we should be. We could have been blown to bits in midair by a bomb placed in our cargo.''

"A few hours ago this Valley of Death became a life raft for us. At least that is what it seemed at first. But it is still true to the name given to it by its inhabitants—the Valley of Death.

"This sandy corridor is part of the Great Rift Valley of Africa. It is like a vast trench formed by the sinking of the earth's crust along a line from Palestine down through the Red Sea, across Ethiopia, Kenya, Mozambique, and out to the Indian ocean.

"This valley is a wild, inhospitable desert. Its soda lakes have undrinkable water. We are surrounded by active volcanoes, to say nothing of a sprinkling of hostile nomads who are known to kill on sight.''

Once more an uneasy tension rippled through the night gathering.

"If help does not come by noon tomorrow, we must take further emergency action. Our food and water supplies are almost nothing. Dr. Ngambu informs me that at least a dozen of his patients cannot survive this desert heat another twenty-four hours.

"I have flown over these escarpments many times. I know there are ravines and cuts in the cliffs made by ancient water flows. Whether we are close to one I do not know. What I propose is that we send out exploration parties—one north and one south—to discover a passable route up to the plateau. A route by which we could transport our litter patients as well as ourselves. There is no guarantee that such a route exists within a feasible range, but I feel that we must find out. Do you agree with me?''

There were a variety of responses, but no one disagreed. The Captain would have to have the skills of a Moses to lead his people on such a hazardous journey, Eric reasoned. But he had the relentless heat on his side as well as the hunger pangs soon to erupt in earnest.

"I want to be very frank with you and assess both our strengths and weaknesses," Captain McGuire continued after he had received a signal he was looking for.

"As most of you know, our cargo manifest revealed a shipment of medical supplies Dr. Ngambu has been putting to good use all day. Without these and the doctor's skills, our fatalities would have tripled.

"The cargo luggage of two of our passengers also contained a small cache of hunting knives, guns, and ammunition. These were properly declared and passed through customs. I will say more about these later."

His listeners sensed the significance of his words. Even if the threats were equally as great, Eric reflected, transfer to the higher ground must be made.

"We have two men who are highly qualified to lead such parties," said the Captain. For the first time sounds of response from the small group had a note of optimism.

"To those of you who haven't already met them, I would like to introduce Dr. David Bjornson and Dr. Lars Schmitt."

A flashlight focused briefly on their faces.

"In spite of their youthfulness, these men are internationally recognized for their knowledge of African wildlife. They are naturalists on their way to do wildlife research in Kenya for the Swedish Institute of

Natural History. It is their equipment that makes our plan a possibility.''

Eric had gained a speaking acquaintance with both of the men. They had been among the most active of the passengers in organizing the camp. Both appeared to be in their late thirties, both large, Viking types. David Bjornson was darkened and tanned from his years of exposure to the African sun. Lars Schmitt, on the other hand, had retained his native fairness of complexion even though his years in Africa had been as many as David's. Eric had found both men pleasant and self-confident. Better still, their sense of humor had not been destroyed by the disaster.

The Captain continued. ''David and Lars will be in complete charge of the parties and will select their own companions. They will give us their decision in the morning.

''We must dismiss now. We cannot count on this privacy for long. But first, I must tell you that one more passenger—Sarah Lander—belongs here with us.'' There was a moment of shocked surprise from his hearers. ''You have seen her walking about clicking her camera and identifying with the disgruntled. She accepted my suggestion to be part of the solution instead of the problem, and we made a deal.

''Right now she is out there doing some listening for me,'' the Captain continued. ''We have reason to believe there are some hostile elements growing within the camp. Sarah's an American. Works for the World News Service out of London. Formerly attached to the American CIA.''

Captain McGuire dismissed the gathering as quickly

as it had begun. Walking back into the darkness toward the camp, Eric sensed that Alison was more shaken than she had been at any time since the crash.

"When the Captain said there were three persons on board who might provoke terrorist acts, he included us, didn't he?" Alison was trembling.

"He may have, Sis, since he said he knew about us from the State Department. I suppose he has to consider us possible targets. The U.S. does have its enemies.

"But I have a strong hunch, Sis, that the black fighter plane was aiming for another target. And for starters, I'd guess he was present in that meeting a few moments ago."

Near exhaustion herself, Alison joined Mary Hastings to help on her midnight rounds. Eric joined them and found his help appreciated. When they finished, he suggested they try to find a place to sleep in the plane.

Alison agreed a little doubtfully. She looked around at all the hurt and frightened people. "I wonder if we won't be needed out here."

"Probably. But we won't be any good if we don't get some sleep ourselves. Let's crash for a little while."

"Eric! What about the briefcase and all the research material we collected for Dad?"

"I haven't even thought about it! It must be where I left it—in the compartment over our seat. It can wait until morning. We can't poke around in the dark."

But Alison was set on recovery. "I won't sleep until I know what has happened to it." She started off toward the jagged break in the plane. "Come on, I've still got the flashlight."

Eric followed. He knew it would be more difficult to persuade her this was ridiculous than it would be to go after the briefcase. Besides, it might comfort her. He knew where it was. It shouldn't take long to get it.

They had spent several days in London's British Museum collecting information their father needed for his work with the International Agricultural Foundation. The twins had assisted him before in collecting materials for his conferences. What he had asked them to do this time was the most important assignment he had ever given them. They knew how valuable the materials in the briefcase would be to their father.

They reached the rear section of the fuselage and climbed up to the broken floor, which was tilted at a sharp angle. Eric flashed the beam of a rescued flashlight slowly about the area where they had been seated. The circle of light revealed broken and dislodged seats. Clothing was strewn about. Hand luggage was broken open and scattered.

"It's spooky," said Alison. "It's like going through a house somebody has ransacked."

"We can come back in the morning." Eric was quick to suggest. "Look out—don't slip on that steep floor."

"No—we've come this far. I wonder why everything is thrown around. It looks like—Eric! Somebody *has* been through here, looting the baggage that was left. What kind of people—?"

Eric felt a sudden anxiety. It was hard to believe anything like this could have happened. He wondered if the Captain knew. He turned the light to look for their seat numbers. Scattered sheets of paper fluttered in the faint breeze coming through the open emergency door.

40

"Our research papers!" Alison cried.

Eric's briefcase had been torn open. Its contents were scattered. Evidently looters had not found anything they considered of value. They merely threw the papers about, scattering them over the cabin floor and seats. Fortunately they had not tossed them out the door. After an hour of persistent searching and sorting, Alison and Eric found all the pages of their work and had arranged them in order.

"Aren't you glad we came?" relieved Alison whispered. "Next time don't argue with your older sister."

Eric was obviously relieved, too. "OK. You win. I'm glad you found your diary, too," he whispered back. "Now let's get some sleep."

Within moments, the twins had located a pair of unoccupied seats and sank down in weariness. Next to the window, Alison could see the moonlight glistening on the edge of the high plateau. She trembled with a sudden chill.

"What's the matter?" Eric asked.

"What if they never find us?"

"Come on, Sis! Don't pull that kind of stuff on me. Of course they'll find us. It would be impossible for them not to. Gramps will use all the muscle he has to keep a search going."

"But shouldn't we have seen at least *one* plane today?"

"Like the Captain says, they've probably run into problems organizing the search. Tomorrow, planes will be buzzing over us like flies."

They huddled down in the seat, but neither of them could find sleep. Every sound seemed amplified by the desert night. The cries and moans of those in pain could not be shut out.

"Do you realize that only this morning we had one of those wonderful English breakfasts in London?" Alison remembered. "Seems unreal that the important things now are the fair distribution of a few dried sandwiches and protection from the desert sun!"

Eric too struggled with repeated thoughts about food. "What do you think was our most important contribution to our survival today?"

It worked. Even a suggestion of humor crept into her voice as she answered.

"Some of the women began to get nervous about toilet facilities. There are no trees to duck behind in this place. I thought about it; then asked a man (that Lars Schmitt the Captain introduced tonight), to help me collect some of those green bushes growing here and there on the desert floor. Those two little boys that sat across the aisle from us thought it was a game and helped a lot.

"We piled the bushes to screen a temporary toilet."

"So you were the architect of that green thing! I can just hear Gramps telling that story to his Washington friends."

Alison enjoyed the subtle compliment and showed it. Finally they slept.

Eric awoke slowly as the sound of someone calling in soft, desperate tones began to register on his sleep-dulled mind. It seemed to be coming from the ground below the open exit door. Everything was dark—very dark.

"Alison—Alison—Oh please come!"

Eric reached over to touch her shoulder. Alison sat up with a start. The anguished calls continued.

"It's Michelle! Oh—something's happened to her baby—"

Alison scrambled out of her seat and along the aisle to the opening where Michelle was standing.

"What is it, Michelle?" asked Alison. Eric appeared beside her.

"Marie—my baby—she's so cold. And I can't wake her—"

Alison and Eric jumped down and ran with Michelle to the other side of the plane. There, under the stars, Laurence Duchene was sitting on the ground rocking his baby back and forth, crooning a French lullaby in a desperate, choked voice.

He held the baby closer as Eric and Alison knelt on the ground beside him. Eric put his arm around the grieving Michelle. Alison began to comfort the father as though he were a child himself.

"He thinks he can bring her back to life," sobbed Michelle.

After a while Laurence let Alison touch the tiny body. There was no question. The baby had been dead for several hours.

"She's dead, isn't she?" Laurence said bitterly. There was no longer any tenderness in his voice.

"I'm so sorry," Eric said. All the words of comfort he could think of seemed terribly flat.

"You're sorry?" Laurence sobbed. "Where's the God we prayed to to make our baby well? What does He care! Don't tell me He's sorry too!" His sudden grief spilled out in angry words and bitter tears.

"Laurence, please—" Michelle knelt and put her head on his shoulder. "Oh Laurence—what if we'd never had our baby at all."

Laurence Duchene gave her a bitter snarl.

Michelle's added grief at being shut off from her husband hurt almost as much as did the death of her child. Alison patted her arm and cried.

Laurence stood up and without any words handed the bundle to Michelle. He headed off into the desert, Eric following.

Laurence stopped abruptly and whirled about.

"I don't want you following me!"

Eric continued to follow at a distance. He wanted desperately to find the right words. To say that God really *was* sorry, too.

"Please help me, Father," Eric prayed silently. "Show me how to help him. He's confused and hurt. And I'm not sure what You want me to do."

Eric continued to follow, and Laurence continued to mumble and cry.

Suddenly, Laurence stopped. He seemed to be waiting for Eric to catch up.

"What's the use of anything?" he demanded angrily. "The devil owns the world and you can't fight back, no matter how you try."

"Should we just give up and turn the world over to him?" Eric asked.

"We don't have to—he's already got it!" Laurence yelled back. "What do you, or I, or anyone have to say about it?"

"Maybe that's why he's got it."

"What do you mean?"

"Well, I believe God always has the last word, even though we don't always understand it. If you don't believe that, then it seems logical to believe Satan's in control."

The Frenchman clenched his fists and turned his face up to the desert stars.

"Our baby's better off out of all this messed up world," he said at last. "And so would be the rest of us."

"Did God create the world for you, or for Satan? I'm sure Satan thinks it's worth fighting for, Laurence, do you?"

The great sobs came again. Laurence pressed his fists to his face.

"Death comes sometimes late—sometimes early," Eric said. "Some of us got an extension on life today. Your baby didn't. But that doesn't mean God is playing favorites. No one escapes death. Jesus showed us that—no matter how terrible—death is not the end—"

"You may be right, Eric," Laurence said after his tears were spent. "But I cry for my little Marie. I cry for my Michelle. I cry for all of us. It's my grief that blocks out God's comfort."

"Michelle needs you, Laurence. She's grieving, too. Let's go back."

They trudged silently through the sand.

"It's well named," Laurence said bitterly. "The Valley of Death."

Just before sunup, they walked a little way from the camp, Michelle tenderly carrying her baby's blanketed body in her arms. Near the desolate site where the other dead had been buried, they scraped a shallow hole in the sand. Laurence laid the small body in the grave and marked the place with a piece of metal from the plane.

As they turned away, they saw the tall dark figure of Dr. Ngambu standing a little way from them.

"I'm so sorry," Dr. Ngambu told the Duchenes, "so very sorry. I would have done anything possible to have saved your baby." For a rare moment his eyes glistened with tears in the morning light. "But there was nothing I could do. Nothing at all—"

Michelle laid her hand on his arm to say she understood the deep feelings of helplessness he was trying to express.

Dr. Ngambu continued to stare at her as if wanting to say something else. But no words came. He turned and plodded wearily, shoulders hunched forward, back toward the camp.

4 • The Doctor's Confession

After a breakfast of dry emergency rations, David Bjornson sought out Eric and Laurence to accompany him on the south leg of the patrol. Lars chose two companions to go north.

Laurence looked gray and grim in the strong morning light, but his body was robust and well-suited for the exploration.

"Are you up to it, Laurence?" Eric asked.

"You were the one who said it is up to us to fight against the evil that is trying to destroy the world. The Valley of Death is a good place to start."

Alison was angry at the suggestion she lacked experience and endurance for such a trip.

"I'm in as good condition as you are, Eric Thorne, and you know it! Convince David—"

Her anger cooled a little when Eric assured her she was right, and finally she agreed the decision was up to David after all. But no one could calm down Mary

Hastings. She exploded at the implication she could not keep up with the men.

"I was tramping the savannahs and jungles of this part of the world when some of you were still in short pants!" She shook her finger in David's face and shouted at him with a merry glint in her eyes. "If you think you can outwalk and outclimb me, I'd like to see you try! Besides, I know these valleys and escarpments. I've lived along them—"

David backed away from the threatening Mary, laughing and putting his hands up before his face in mock fear. "I give up! I apologize! You are welcome to go," he exclaimed.

Alison gave Eric a triumphant look but said nothing.

Mary put her hands on her hips and stood her ground. "Well, why don't we get started? We should have been on our way two hours ago!"

"We're leaving," David nodded, still smiling. "As soon as Charles gives us our rations."

Mary Hastings was the best equipped of any except David and Lars. She had clothes and shoes for trekking through jungle or desert. The rest of them donned what they had by way of rough shirts and jeans and walking shoes. They tied protective scarves of torn cloth about their heads like makeshift Bedouin headgear.

Small packs of food were distributed, along with plastic bottles of water. David and Lars carried high-powered rifles, and it was agreed a signal of three shots would indicate to the other that an ascent path had been found.

Eric found it hard to leave Alison. Deeper than her resentment about not being allowed to go was her concern about the sudden change in their situation. Now she was concerned about Dad's worrying in Capetown about them. The change from expecting immediate rescue to the new fear that it might be a considerable time away—or not at all—had unnerved her.

"Remember what Dad always used to say when we were kids and the going got tough?" Eric asked.

Alison nodded, clinging close. "I know. 'Dig in and pull harder.' "

"Twinny, you've been doing great. This is a tough one. We'll be back as soon as we find a stairway in that cliff that some natives built a thousand years ago just for us! Captain McGuire needs you here. See if you can talk old Jakob Vroorman into liking the Doctor!"

The two parties moved out quickly. Already the air was swirling in hot blasts and stirring dust devils along the valley floor. The two exploring parties would be in the long shadow of the eastern wall of the Valley until almost midmorning.

David's party had gone about a mile when they came to a small turn in the wall of the escarpment that brought into view additional areas of the Valley. Mary Hastings paused a moment and shaded her eyes, squinting into the far distance. Eric could see nothing ahead but the same desolation that was behind them.

"You see something, Miss Hastings?" asked David.

"The name is Mary, and I shall call you David, since you were kind enough to allow me along. Yes, I do see something. Those birds—"

David squinted into the distance.

"I see them circling way out there."

Eric and Laurence followed his gaze. They were not sure they saw anything at all.

"Do they tell you anything?" asked Mary.

"Something on the ground interests them."

"Water," said Mary. "There is most likely a pond or even a small lake of drinkable water that attracts the birds."

"Possibly," said David. "It would be good to have a supply of water available, and we could use the birds for food."

"You miss my point," said Mary. "If there's water, how did it get there?"

"From a spring, perhaps. What does that have to do with our problem?"

"It is likely fed from a flow off the plateau, which means very possibly an eroded gorge that would provide a path to the top. I've seen scores of such places along the edge of the Rift."

David had been watching the increasing whiteness of the desert closely. Occasionally, he raised his field glasses and scanned the forbidding landscape ahead. Near noon he paused and passed the glasses to Mary. "What kind of birds are they?" he asked.

Mary took the glasses.

"Flamingoes," she said finally. "A soda lake." She lowered the glasses. "That still doesn't mean there can't be an eroded gorge in the side of the cliff, feeding the lake."

"No. It just makes it more unlikely."

Eric felt exasperated. "You're talking way over my head. I don't understand."

David explained, "Many lakes in the Rift Valley are

saturated with soda. They breed a green algae which provides food especially suited to a certain species of flamingoes. There are more of them here in the Rift Valley than in all the rest of the world—over three million.

"Such a soda lake is more likely very stagnant, often fed from underground springs, without any input from the plateau. So the inference that an eroded side valley may be nearby is not very strong."

Across the Valley, thirty miles away, the western escarpment was not nearly so steep. It looked quite possible to climb those hills, but the thirty-mile trek was out of the question.

The nearby cliffs still towered almost straight up. Laurence stared about him. "The pictures of the moon —the astronauts walking on it. It wasn't any more desolate than this."

"If any of you feel like going back," said David, "it's all right. There's no telling how far we might have to go to find a break in the wall. Ten miles— twenty-five—fifty—"

"I think ten miles has to be our absolute limit," said Eric. "Even if we found an ascent farther than that, we couldn't get our people to it."

"Our lives depend on doing what we have to do," said David. "Who knows how much that is?"

They swallowed a mouthful of water and ate a tiny chunk of aging sandwich and moved on. The floor of the Valley grew whiter. Salt pillars, like enormous inverted icicles ten to twenty feet high, began to rise here and there. They were layered with thousands of small tiers.

There was no letup on the baking, searing heat. And the small wind was even an enemy. It whipped up the soda dust so that it caked on their bodies. They held the ends of their head scarves to their faces, trying to filter out the burning dust.

Eric's eyes traced the edge of the plateau above. He could see the faint movement of tree branches, and longed for the touch of that cool breeze that moved them. It had to be cool, he thought, at least in comparison with the hot blast that surrounded them.

Through the remainder of the day, the endless wall stretched ahead to seeming infinity. It was the wall of some maze in which they were trapped like white rats, Eric thought. The distant lake and the occasional cloud of birds seemed to grow no nearer. They estimated they had covered ten to twelve miles.

The sun was low on the western plateau when David called a halt. He scanned the escarpment with his glasses, then slowly lowered them, shaking his head.

"There's nothing in sight. We hadn't planned to be gone overnight, but we're too far to return before dark. I suggest we keep going, then stop for the night and return tomorrow."

Discouraged by their failure, the rest agreed. In the remaining light they moved on. No planes had been seen or heard over the Valley throughout each day. Something *was* wrong that no searchers had come. Each of them understood now—and they knew the people back at camp understood—that finding a way out of the Valley was not just something nice to have in case they needed it. They *did* need it. It was necessary that a way be found.

Yet, ahead of them—nothing.

Just as before they were ready to call a halt for the day, Laurence suddenly raced ahead. In a kind of frenzy he ran to a spot on the cliff.

Then the rest of them saw it, too. A trickle of water flowing down the red and yellow walls.

"Wait!" David called. "Don't drink that!"

Laurence put his hands under the trickle and guided it over his face and arms and let it flow into his mouth. David broke into a run and knocked him away. Laurence fell to the sand.

"How do you know it's bad?" said Eric.

The sight of the water was an agonizing temptation to him, too.

"I don't," said David, "but if it is it could kill him—very painfully."

Laurence raised himself from the sand, his face angry and bewildered. Eric moved quickly to his side.

"I'm sorry," said David. "You just don't lap up the water in places like this without checking it first."

"It felt so cool—and tasted so good," said Laurence wearily.

The little stream looked clear. David wet his finger in it and touched it cautiously to his tongue. He tried it again.

"Very little mineral," he said. "It must be coming straight down from the top. This could be a water supply for the camp—if we don't make it out of the Valley."

"If we don't make it out, we won't need much of a water supply," said Mary.

David put his arm about the missionary's shoulders.

"Mary," he said, "you could have gone all day without saying that." Then he added more seriously. "But of course you're quite right—which means we will make it out and won't worry about this as our water supply. OK?"

"Of course," said Mary quietly. "You're entirely right."

They were not prepared to camp for the night, but they scooped hollows in the sand and lay down under the tropic stars. Eric stared up at their brilliance. They seemed like a link to the outside world. His father, in Capetown, could see those same stars. In London, some of them could be seen. Yet here in this forbidding desert he and Alison and all their companions were as cut off from the rest of the world as if they were on another planet.

He felt more depressed than at any time since the crash. It seemed as if that had occurred years ago instead of just yesterday. Why had there been no searchers? Were they looking somewhere else? How could they possibly be looking anywhere but along the course the airliner was on?

He slept, along with the others, for a short time. He awoke dreaming he heard shooting. He thought for a moment he was back on the 747 and the black plane was firing. Then he knew it wasn't that. It was a single, faraway shot, so faint it was almost beyond the reach of hearing.

Then another. And, after a count of ten, one more.

It was the signal that the north party had found an ascent up the escarpment.

Eric's companions stirred.

"I knew our prayers would be answered," said Mary fervently. "It was good there were two parties."

"How could we hear a gunshot that far away?" said Eric. "If they have traveled as far as we have, they are twenty-five miles from us, at least."

"These are some pretty big guns Lars and I carry," said David. "They can stop a rampaging elephant in one shot. And this Valley with its high walls acts like a big pipe. It'll carry the sound a long way."

"I'll bet they're back at the camp," said Eric. "They returned and found we weren't there, so they gave the signal again. They'd already given it during the day, and we *didn't* hear them."

"You may be right," said David, impressed with the young American.

They tried to sleep again. Eric was next to David. He could tell the naturalist was not sleeping soundly.

"You asleep?" Eric whispered, after a while.

"Yeah—and you'd better get some shut-eye, too."

"Have you figured out the attack on our plane?"

"Not much chance of doing that with what little we know."

"The way I figure it, there are two kinds of terrorist attacks," said Eric. "One is a random attack against any nearby target just to cause damage and fear. The other is an attack aimed at some specific target with the intent to destroy it for a definite purpose."

"So—what are you getting at?"

"Which kind of attack was ours?"

"It could have been either," said David. "I tend to agree with McGuire's theory. With the elaborate setup of a well-equipped fighter plane shooting down a commercial flight rather than planting a bomb aboard or attacking on the ground—I have no doubt someone on this airplane was a specific target."

"There are lots of easier ways to kill an individual."

"Terrorists like to be spectacular," said David. "But where does that get us?"

"I think in order to understand the seriousness of our situation, we have to know which passenger was the object of the attack."

"And whether we can expect further complications?"

"Right. And we have the question of why no search planes have appeared. They would have been absolutely certain to search the flight corridor the 747 was in unless—"

"Unless what?"

"Unless they were deliberately steered somewhere else."

"And how would you explain that?" asked David. Up to this point he had followed Eric's theory with interest. Now the boy seemed to be getting a little carried away.

"It could have happened if the terrorists had an accomplice in the Nairobi control who would misdirect the search."

"Boy, you really have got it figured out!" teased David. Then he added soberly. "But you might be right. You just might be entirely right, Eric."

At the first light of morning they started the journey back to camp. They were stiff from lying on the hard sand, but they limbered up after a few minutes of walking. They drank again from the trickle of water falling down from the cliff face and filled their plastic bottles.

The Valley was ghostlike in the dawn. The faint glow in the sky did not yet light up the depths between the great cliffs. It was like walking through some dark passage with only the promise of light from above. But soon the sun came up, and the heat returned.

"That Bedouin headgear looks pretty good on you, Laurence," Eric quipped as they strode along rapidly, anxious to get back to camp and begin the move to the plateau.

Laurence smiled.

"I'm keeping my ears covered today. Got them burned yesterday. Heard any planes?"

Eric shook his head. He was more convinced than ever that he was right, that someone in Nairobi was deliberately misdirecting the search. A fantastic theory, he had to admit. But no more fantastic than their being shot down in the first place. After all, it was the third day since the crash.

"I wonder what kind of a trail they found," remarked Mary to David.

"It's bound to have a lot of problems. We'll have to send up a party to set up a base camp and prepare for the injured. Some of the litter cases may have to be hoisted by ropes. Lars and I are pretty optimistic about it. Our survival depends on it."

Mary was equally certain of their success.

It was late afternoon when they reached camp. Alison spotted them a long way off and walked to meet them. She threw her arms about Eric. He could feel her trembling.

"I was so worried!" she cried. "You didn't say you were going to be gone so long—and then the others came back."

Eric hugged her close and patted her shoulder.

"I'm sorry, Sis. We didn't know. We just kept looking, and we didn't find anything."

Alison dried her eyes and smiled up at Eric.

"I'm sorry I was such a silly. I just got scared last night. The heat, the dark, that *wall*. I just got the feeling we'll never make it out of here."

"How about Lars' group? We heard their shots. Did they say what they found?"

"They showed us pictures they took," Alison reported as they resumed the hike toward the camp. "It looks awful. I don't see how we've got a chance of making it up the route they found."

"It's got to be better than what we came up with. There's not a break in the wall for at least twenty miles to the south."

David spoke up. "Did Lars give any details of how he thought the climb could be made?"

"He's been planning with Captain McGuire and Dr. Ngambu and some of the others all day. It looks nearly impossible to me."

"Sometimes an impossible thing has to be done," said David grimly.

Eric squeezed Alison's hand.

"You and I have been in places this tight before. We made it then. We'll make it now."

"I know. Sometimes I just need you to tell me about it."

"It's good we have David and Lars with us."

"And Mary Hastings, and Captain McGuire, and Dr. Ngambu. We have a lot of good people pulling together. We'll get out of this hole."

Michelle, too, had been worried. She greeted Laurence with tearful joy. And Captain McGuire welcomed them all.

"After you have time to rest, David, I want you to see the pictures Lars' group brought back and listen to the plans discussed so far."

David listened and stared at the pictures.

"It will be more difficult than I thought, but I agree it has to be attempted. There's no time to look for an easier route. Like Lars, I think the first scouting party should consist of a dozen people. Instead of everyone coming back down, half should remain on top and prepare a camp, find game and water. The others can return and bring down some game for food, and then get the rest of the camp moving in relays. We should be able to move everybody in three days, I'd say."

"Including the injured?" Eric asked.

"If we can find a half decent route up that cliff. If we have to hoist the injured by rope and stretcher over many spots, it could take longer."

"In three days we will lose many patients," said Dr. Ngambu.

Sarah Lander ranted about the stupidity of anyone who would attempt such a climb. She insulted Captain McGuire, who patiently brushed her aside. She buttonholed other passengers singly or in groups, yakking at anyone who would listen.

Eric stood back watching her. He was glad this negative, complaining attitude was not her permanent nature.

Later that evening, in the light of the fire that had been built of brush and aging logs washed down from above, Eric moved toward the journalist as she stood alone. For the moment, she was not complaining.

"It seems a little more hopeful tonight," said Eric, "now that we have found a way to the top."

Sarah Lander quickly put her mask back on. "You think any of us are going to make it up that mountain goat path? It's absolutely insane to think of such a thing!"

Eric watched her. She appeared to be intelligent, sensitive, and sophisticated. But she kept her mask up.

"Sarah Lander, I know your act is phony," Eric said. "Why don't you drop it?"

The lady looked taken aback. This young man was using her own tactics.

"I know who you are. I remembered as soon as The Captain mentioned your name to me. I've read the columns of Sarah Lander on political and international news for my current events class. I know the writer of those columns is no fool, no complaining cub reporter. So, you may fool the yokels in the balcony with that act you're using, but from here in the front row it's as phony as a politician's campaign promise."

Sarah burst out laughing until she had to move away to the shadows to keep from attracting attention. Eric followed her.

"It's a long time since anyone called Sarah Lander a phony and got away with it," she said. "But who isn't a phony? That's the first thing you learn in the newspaper business. Everybody puts up a front for others to see. Anyway, I keep the troops stirred up."

"Don't kid me, and I won't kid you, OK?"

She looked at Eric hard for a long moment. Then her smile died and she grew serious.

"All right, Eric Thorne, I'll level with you—"

"How do you know who I am?" Eric interrupted.

She laughed. "As you said, don't kid me and I won't kid you. Your father's mission is certainly news, you know. And you have a rather special grandfather in Washington if I am not mistaken."

The young man was a little shaken.

"I'm in Africa to find out about the new president of the African state of Niroona. He's going to be a very important man in the future of this continent."

"The new president of Niroona? What are you talking about?"

"Don't you know? I thought Eric Thorne knew all the inside international developments about where he travels."

"I tell you I don't know anything. I didn't even know there was a new president."

"You haven't been doing your homework lately. Didn't you ever hear of a certain Dr. Alfred Ngambu?"

"Ngambu!" Eric felt stunned.

He certainly hadn't been paying enough attention to what was going on in Africa. Niroona was a newly formed nation sitting in the middle of the continent on top of incredible wealth in gold, copper, diamonds and cobalt. A dozen factions, both inside and outside the country, had been struggling to get their hands on this wealth.

"So Dr. Ngambu was the compromise candidate—with powerful enemies against him."

"So who do you think that black plane was shooting at?" said Sarah.

Here it was at last—the missing piece of the puzzle. And to think this surprising woman knew it all the time. Alison must be told. Part of her new distress was the thought that just maybe their presence might have triggered this ghastly disaster.

His thoughts sped to the distinguished Doctor.

"But Dr. Ngambu is a *good* man."

"Right. And in this world it's the good guys that get shot at—first!"

Dr. Ngambu had slept hardly at all since the crash. He was constantly on the move from one patient to another, changing bandages, checking injuries, administering sedatives, just talking and comforting them. He even tried to talk to old Jakob Vroorman, but the Afrikaner closed his eyes and turned his face away whenever the Doctor came near.

Eric approached as Dr. Ngambu neared the end of his evening round. The Doctor was exhausted.

"I want to tell you how much I admire your persistence in caring for these people," Eric said. "But you ought to take some time out for yourself."

The Doctor smiled tiredly as he straightened and adjusted the glasses on his nose.

"Thank you for your kindness, Eric," he said. "I'll rest when these people are safe again. My work is not a burden. It is part of my discharging of my debt, the debt every man owes the moment he is born."

In the flickering firelight the Doctor's ebony features seemed majestic.

"It would be a wonderful world if all men felt a need to pay their debts," said Eric with new understanding.

"Indeed it would."

"I have just learned that you are repaying in still another way, Dr. Ngambu, that you have just been elected president of your country."

The Doctor was suddenly wide awake. Dismay flooded his handsome features.

"Ah, so you know. Captain McGuire assured me it was best to keep my new political identity hidden as long as possible. You see, all this happened because of me." His glance took in the whole camp and lingered on those who were his medical charges.

"Your enemies tried to destroy you."

Dr. Ngambu nodded. "And they cared nothing about destroying all these innocent people as well. You see why I cannot rest. All these—" he swept a hand over the injured—"are part of my debt. Such a great debt! And my opponents are terrible—insane—vicious —powerful. I doubt that I shall complete my term of office. But a man must do what he has to do."

"There must be a way to fight them."

"If I can gain the support of enough good men both within my country and without, perhaps I shall have a chance. It is the weakness of otherwise good men, however, that they so often avoid conflict, and thus evil and reckless men become the victors."

He sighed deeply and looked about once more. "But if you have learned of my appointment, then others have also. It is only fair that I make my peace with them all.''

He struggled to his feet and moved toward the firelight. For a moment Eric didn't understand what was happening. Suddenly he knew. The Doctor raised his hands for attention. The buzz of conversation in a dozen languages slowly quieted.

Dr. Ngambu spoke in French, the language understood by most of the passengers. He called to one of the stewardesses to repeat what he had said in English.

''You have all wondered about the senseless, brutal attack on our airplane. I should have eased your minds long ago, but I allowed the Captain to convince me that this painful confession would not be required of me. I have come to see, however, that it must be so.

''I am the one who was the object of the attack.''

5 • *Assassination Plot*

Gasps of surprise and dismay—and sudden, sharp mutterings of anger—rose from the group. Eric was startled at the hateful oaths he heard in nearby whispers.

"Some of you know—and this is the reason I felt compelled to speak," Dr. Ngambu continued, "that I have had the honor to be called to be President of my poor country, Niroona. I say poor because it is poor in spirit and unity and purpose. But it is rich in newly discovered wealth of the earth. Greedy and selfish men are grasping for this wealth, and because I desire to keep it out of their hands and use it for the benefit of all of my people, these men would kill me. They would also kill scores of the innocent, to be sure I was destroyed.

"My sorrow is deep. I would not knowingly have brought this tragedy upon any of you. I would willingly have given my life to these evil men to have spared you the suffering I have caused. I shall continue to do all in

66

my power to make amends. I ask forgiveness from each of you."

As Dr. Ngambu stepped away from the fire, he was surrounded by those who embraced him and assured him they bore him no blame. But Eric noted there were many who did not go up to him but who huddled in small groups that moved closer together, heads bent down in angry conversation.

"Why did you do it, Doctor?" an anguished Captain McGuire asked the African. Eric waited for the answer that would blame him.

"It is of no matter, Captain. The time had come," Ngambu said.

Eric moved away and looked for Alison, who was sitting with Michelle and Laurence against the fuselage in the darkness.

"The Doctor is a wonderful man," Michelle murmured.

"I've got to talk to you, Alison," Eric said quietly. As they hurried out of earshot, Alison could see that her twin was deeply troubled. Sick at heart, he told her that he was the one who had triggered the Doctor's confession, perhaps even at the risk of the man's life.

It was impossible now to ignore the angry reactions of the little groups of whispering passengers. Eric feared that Captain McGuire would no longer be able to protect the Doctor as he had hoped.

"You thought it would be something like this, didn't you?" Alison asked.

Eric nodded, feeling sick at the thought of all the feelings he had caused to be stirred up among the passengers.

"He didn't have to say anything," Eric shook his head sadly. "His secret was safe with me!"

They fell silent, Eric regretting what had happened. Alison shared his pain.

Out of the shadows Sarah Lander suddenly descended on Eric in fury. "You fool! You utter fool! What have you done? They'll kill him now. Don't you know that? They'll kill him."

Michelle and Laurence, hearing the outburst, hurried to join the twins.

Eric, protested, retreating from Sarah's fury. "I didn't mean for him to get up and confess to the whole camp. I didn't even suggest such a thing."

"You should have known what he would do when he realized people knew who he was and that he was the object of the attack! Now they will kill him."

"What do you mean by 'they'?" Alison demanded, angry now at Sarah's attack on Eric. "Who will want to kill Dr. Ngambu?"

"Remember, I keep informed. It could be that black fellow that keeps playing his guitar fourteen hours a day. It could be that fat millionaire who sleeps with a cigar in his mouth. It could be those two fellows wearing turbans who are always whispering together. That group of oil sheiks. Or even that little lady who sits against the fuselage with her knitting all day."

Sarah shook her head at their innocence.

"I've talked to them all. They're bitter and just aching for a fall guy. You just don't understand that many of these people will believe now that it is a matter of honor to destroy Dr. Ngambu. They blame him for the attack, not the terrorists. It's like the old days of so-called chivalry. If a man stepped on your toe, you were honor bound to draw your sword and challenge him to a duel to the death right on the spot.''

"Oh, you're just being dramatic! We don't live in that kind of world any more!'' Alison exclaimed.

"Want to bet on that?'' Sarah's voice was bitter. "There are at least two dozen people here who will decide that they can live in honor only if Ngambu dies. He is a Jonah who has brought evil upon them. Like Jonah of the Old Testament, he must be thrown into the sea so that the whole ship won't be lost.''

"That's insane!''

"Insane to you. Logic to them. One man's insanity is another man's logic.''

Eric and the Duchenes were silent. They understood what Sarah was saying.

"I don't see why he did it," said Michelle. "Surely he knew—''

"I'm sure he knows," said Eric. "He told me that if I knew who he really was, others did also. Maybe plenty of the others already knew.''

"That doesn't change anything," said Sarah. "His life is in danger.''

"Then we'll protect him," said Eric. "We'll see that nothing happens to him before we're rescued.''

"And just how are you going to do that?'' Sarah asked scornfully.

"We'll watch him, guard him every moment. We'll get others to help.''

"We must let the Captain know," said Alison.

Eric hesitated, then he said, "No— I don't think we should bother Captain McGuire with this.''

"Bother!" exclaimed Sarah. "You're talking about a good man's life!"

"The Captain's responsible for a couple of hundred lives," said Eric. "He's got more than his load now. Besides, he's hurting. That wound on his head must be giving him a bad time. Let's get David and Lars to help. Maybe they'll have some ideas. I'm really sick about the problem I've caused. Help me handle it without putting more of a load on the Captain. Please, Sarah?"

"All right—if you can get David and Lars to agree also. They're tough enough to handle this." Her insinuations were not lost on Eric.

Later, when Eric and Sarah spoke to David and Lars, the naturalists scoffed at the idea that Dr. Ngambu could be assassinated because he was regarded as a Jonah aboard the plane. But Sarah finally convinced them, and they agreed to be responsible for a watch over the Doctor without burdening the Captain with this additional worry.

The Doctor was not to know he was being guarded. In addition to whatever protection the Captain had already arranged, David and Lars casually laid their bedrolls next to the spot where he slept. The Doctor finally turned in, wishing them a pleasant good night.

David was to watch the first half of the night, Lars the second. Whenever they were out of range, Laurence was to take over the watch.

Morning came quickly, blazing with heat. Eric rose at the first touch of sunlight on the ridge of the western cliffs. He saw that David and Lars and Captain McGuire were already up and conferring about a plan for scaling the escarpment.

As Eric moved to join them, David said, "We should send four men back to the spring we found. The plane's water tanks could be torn out and put on a sled of sheet metal. Enough water could be brought back to see us through the climb to the top."

The Captain agreed. "We'll get them started right away."

"For the rest of it," David said, "the plan we decided on yesterday will be followed. Half our party will remain on top. The others will return to guide the rest of the camp. We'll work out the problems of getting the injured people up as we go along."

"Dr. Ngambu will want to be with every patient that goes up," said Eric.

"There's only one of him," David responded. "We can't let him spread himself too thin."

"I'd like to go with you," said Eric hopefully.

David looked at him intently for a moment. "I'd like to have you. I'd intended asking you—until last night. If you go, it has to be understood that I am in charge—" He hesitated long enough for Eric to catch his meaning.

"I think Laurence could handle our assignment for one night," he said finally. "We'll arrange for more help when we get back."

Work began while the scanty breakfast was being distributed by the stewards. The four volunteers who were to go to the spring were briefed by David. Others were tearing out the plane's water tanks and preparing skids from sheet metal on which the tanks could be dragged back after they were filled at the spring. Electric cables were torn out to use to drag the skids.

Members of the exploring party had been selected the afternoon before. Final preparations were now completed. The camp was still in the shadow of the eastern cliffs when David and Lars led their group out. Each man carried a half sandwich and a small plastic bottle of water.

In addition to David, Lars, and Eric, there were three young Englishmen, a Frenchman, three Arabs from Middle East countries, and two Africans—twelve in all.

Laurence had agreed to guard Dr. Ngambu closely. He claimed considerable experience with guns, and Lars lent him a pistol. Eric felt satisfied that the Doctor was safe with Laurence on watch near him.

The gorge they would climb was about eight miles north of the camp. The party reached it while they were still in the shadow of the escarpment, but as they entered the mouth of the gorge, the sun's rays edged over the cliff with torch-like heat. The party halted in the shade of an overhanging rock while they allowed themselves the first sip of water since leaving camp.

Eric felt a sinking within him as he looked up the rugged slope leading to the distant plateau. It was a water-worn gorge, true enough, but no great amount of water had flowed down it for a long time. Probably only in time of very heavy runoff—which occurred no more than once in a decade—did any stream flow down those crags. Yet, over many thousands of years, the gorge had been carved.

One of the Englishmen, a fellow named Ralph Botts, stood beside Eric, looking up at the forbidding route. "I'd say it looks a bit rugged, wouldn't you?"

Eric nodded agreement as he felt despair creeping in his own mind. "Yeah—rugged. It sure is."

David and Lars had been discussing plans together. They moved out of the shadow of the rock.

"All right, men," David said in a voice of command. "You see what's ahead of us. It's no picnic for sure. For those of us accustomed to mountain climbing it offers no real difficulty, but we've got to find a route and blaze a trail that can be followed by the women, the children, the older people, and all those who are not mountain climbers. We're going to divide into two groups, one led by Lars and one by myself. This is simply for convenience so we won't be bunched up in the tight spots. I'll take five of you and lead out. Lars and the other five will follow a hundred yards or so behind. Any questions?"

Nobody asked any, but the little groups of different nationalities murmured in their own languages, gloomily shaking their heads. David and Lars exchanged wry smiles.

"Off we go!" said David.

Eric, Ralph Botts, a second Englishman named Jim Southwick, and two of the Arabs accompanied David.

The sun had already heated the rocks and sand and clay of the gorge, and the air within it swirled upward like the blast of a furnace. Jim Southwick, a tall, bony man of about twenty-five, was soon gasping for air. The blast of heat seemed to shrivel the scanty meat on his bones even further.

"We can't make it with only this much water!" he protested.

David paused. "You may go back if you wish. The

next time up we can be allowed more water—if the teams get back from the springs with a supply. For now, the only water is what's in the little bottle, and I expect you to drink from it only when I give permission. That applies to everybody. So—are you staying or going? Jim? Anyone else?"

Jim said, "I'm sorry. I'll make it. It's just that it hits you all at once."

"Yes, that's right. And it keeps hitting all the way."

No one else said anything.

"All right. Let's get moving."

For nearly a mile they followed the smooth, sandy floor of the gorge. It narrowed to a V, and then they were at the edge of the jagged slope. Here they paused and scanned the crags for the best approach. David began to climb.

The clay was soft and crumbly. The footing was treacherous, especially when they stepped from a rock surface onto the clay. Eric followed David carefully, trying to step where the naturalist stepped. As they rounded a narrow ledge, Eric lost his balance a moment and brought his foot down on a clay protrusion at the edge of the rock he was crossing. The clay crumbled beneath his weight.

Eric was winded and scratched and bruised in his fall but otherwise unhurt. He stood for a moment with David looking down at the tracks of his slide. The lone bush that he had caught himself on was the only one within hundreds of feet. Below it was a continuing slope of several hundred additional feet, ending in a precipice that dropped yet another hundred feet to the floor of the gorge.

He took a deep breath. "Somebody must have been praying for me!" he said with sincere thankfulness.

"This has got to be one of your better days," David agreed.

The group turned and retraced their steps half a mile to the rock David had mentioned. The others seemed more shaken by Eric's narrow escape than he did. Most of them were depressed by the gloomy prospects of finding a safe way up.

As they grumbled among themselves, David said again, "Anybody who wants to go back to camp is free to do so. We may die trying to find a way up, and we may die when we get there. But it's certain we'll die if we remain below in that heat and without food."

The grumbling died down.

Eric's frequent glances at the sky were becoming a habit. There was nothing to see. It was certain now that any rescue efforts were being conducted in the wrong area.

David led the way up the other side of the rock pillar. This route took them far to the left of their previous attempt. While the beginning seemed more difficult, it soon became much more passable than the other route, and they advanced several hundred feet in elevation in a short time. Eric began to feel more hopeful. Most of the people could make it this far.

"David!"

Eric cried out involuntarily and threw his arms in the air in a futile struggle for balance. He fell, tumbling, rolling, sliding in a suffocating cloud of powder clay. Scarcely conscious of his actions, he twisted his body as he approached a thin clump of brush growing from the hillside. He struck it and clung. A torrent of clay and dust swept past him.

"Eric!" David's voice sounded a thousand miles away.

He managed to wave a hand, indicating he was all right. He twisted his body about and looked back up the slope. His eyes, blinded with dust, could see a fuzzy image of David, so far away, on the edge above. David seemed to be fussing with some object Eric couldn't quite make out. Then he saw a loop of rope twisting through the air toward him. It landed a few feet above him.

He struggled to get his feet against the feeble stalks of brush. They would never hold. He had to cling with his hands.

"Need six more feet!" he shouted.

David waved and drew back the rope a way. Eric saw that he was tying two lines together. Then it came down again, a loop that he was able to slip over his shoulders and under his arms. He waved and let go of the bush as he felt the tug from above.

David and the two Englishmen helped him over the edge, where he lay a moment panting with exhaustion.

"This route's no good," Eric said finally. "We can't bring the whole camp this way."

David agreed. He called to those in Lars' group.

"We can't go this way. Let's go back to that large pillar of rock and go up the other side of it."

They came to a point where two possible routes formed a Y. The one on the right passed over a broad ledge overlooking the Valley below. A few hundred yards away it passed under a massive clay overhang.

The other route led upward between jagged pinnacles. David turned to the left.

"Wait a minute!" Jim Southwick called out. "Why are we going this way? The path to the right looks much easier."

"That large overhang," David said. He pointed in the direction of the huge mass. "A very slight disturbance could cause it to come down. I wouldn't want to risk taking our people that way."

"That's complete nonsense," Jim said. He was breathing in heavy gasps from the exertion of the climb. "That formation has been there for the last ten thousand years. It's not going to collapse just because we're here. I say we should go that way."

"And I say I'm leading this party. I'm looking for a path on which we can safely bring up our people. That isn't it."

"I'll prove it to you!" Jim Southwick seemed almost irrational to Eric in his sudden rebellion against David's judgment.

"I think we'd better follow David," said Eric quietly. "He's had a lot more experience in this kind of country than any of the rest of us."

"Well, it's nonsense to go through that stuff over there," he waved a hand toward the field of jagged pinnacles, "when we can just as well take the easy way around."

"You may go any way you like," said David, "but I will not take our people that way. Nor will I be responsible for digging you out of any trouble you get into. Go that way and you're on your own."

Eric gripped Jim Southwick's arm.

77

"Don't risk it. Stay with the group, Jim."

The Englishman jerked away from Eric.

"I'll join you on up—maybe at the top. There's more than one head around here that knows how to climb a hill." He called out to the others. "Anybody want to go along with me?"

After a moment's hesitation, the two Arabs in David's group moved in Jim Southwick's direction.

"This is my last warning," said David. "I will not be responsible for you."

They turned and moved away.

David sighed in disgust and turned to the steep, narrow way between the pinnacles. The air was utterly still, and hotter than at any previous time during their climb. The rocks were even too hot to touch. The party moved slowly, winding their way as if through a maze until they reached a small rock plateau. They paused for a rest. There was a faint movement of air.

David looked above, shading his eyes as he surveyed the edge of the plateau against the blue sky. He suddenly grasped Eric's arm.

"We *are* going to make it. I can see a way from here clear to the top."

Eric's eyes followed David's pointing finger. It looked as if the naturalist was right.

"We ought to be able to make that with the stretcher cases, too."

In a burst of enthusiasm, David slapped him on the shoulder. "We've got it made!"

At that moment a rumble like thunder started somewhere just below them. It grew in volume until it sounded like a freight train bearing down at full speed.

"Slide—!" exclaimed Eric. "The overhang—"

A massive plume of gray dust swirled up from beyond the rise behind them. Eric began scrambling back down the way they had come.

"Easy—!" David shouted in warning.

Eric checked himself and descended more cautiously. The others followed, winding their way again through the maze of pillars. Eric came to the point of the Y, where Jim Southwick and his companions had separated from the group. He stared at the path they had taken. A few hundred yards away it no longer existed. David came up behind Eric.

"The overhang—," said Eric.

"It was nothing but a mass of clay, riddled with water cracks. It was ready to go anytime. Their passing was just enough disturbance to trigger it."

The ledge was completely buried for a distance of two hundred feet or more. Boulders and chunks of the mountain continued to pour over the edge to the slopes far below.

"I wonder if they went over the edge," said Eric.

"That—or they're buried under that mass on the ledge. Either way, they're gone."

Ralph Botts shook his head sadly.

"Jim had a bullheaded streak in him, but I never thought—"

"This country makes no allowance for bullheadedness," said Lars. "You learn to respect its strengths, and it will respect yours. That's the only way you can survive."

Sobered by the disaster, they turned once more to the path back through the maze to the small plateau. It's terrible how you can almost get used to death, Eric mused as they continued the slow, painful climb.

The last few hundred feet were actually easier than the beginning. The slope became more gentle, and a small current of air drifted off the high plateau, a few degrees cooler than the air of the gorge.

In the late afternoon the shadows were already filling the Valley below them, but sunlight still filtered through the grove of acacia trees that crowded the edge of the plain onto which they had emerged.

David was the first over the last small incline. He gave Eric a hand and pulled him up. Ralph Botts followed and flung himself on the ground and patted it with heartfelt gladness.

"We made it out of that blasted oven!" he exclaimed, as if he had never believed they would. "We really did!"

Lars touched him gently with his shoe.

"Yes—and tomorrow we're going right back down into it."

"That's all right. As long as I know there's a way out—!"

Eric looked about the landscape to which they had come. The top of the escarpment was quite flat for a distance in all directions. It was a typical African savannah of tall grass and scattered groves of acacia trees.

Beyond, mountains rose into the distant sky. And the highest—Eric stared at it with a twinge of fearful recognition. The top of it was flat, slightly saucer shaped—a volcano. Dead, of course—there was no sign of eruption in recent times. But he had heard about the intense volcanic activity that had raged in the Valley, and its nearby mountains.

Below the plateau, the brown scar of the Valley stretched endlessly in both directions. It looked what it was—utterly dead. Filling now with the dark shadows of night, it was like a place no living thing ought to enter.

Alison was down there, Eric thought. And a couple of hundred others who were looking for a way to survive.

"We'll bed down here for the night," said David. "Lars and I are going to see if we can get an antelope for supper and some meat to take back down. A couple of hind quarters roasted just right ought to make the people in camp feel a lot stronger for the climb. They could use a piece of good steak in their stomachs."

They allowed themselves another sip of water and finished the crumbs of the sandwiches. If David and Lars were successful in their hunt, there would be meat before they went back. Otherwise, there would be nothing.

While it was still light they gathered some of the tall grass for pads to lie upon. After a half hour they heard a distant shot, then another.

"I hope their aim was good," said Ralph. "A steak would taste good tonight, even without the trimmings."

Before twilight vanished they built a fire, in readiness for David and Lars who soon appeared bearing the carcass of an antelope over their shoulders. Slices of meat were cooked on sticks held over the fire. To Eric it tasted better than any meal he had ever eaten.

The nine men took turns on watch to keep the fire going during the night to ward off animals. David and Lars believed they were in very active lion country, although no lions had been seen so far.

All were awake at the first light of dawn—while the Valley was still in deep shadows. Their breakfast of antelope cold cuts brought new strength.

It was decided that Lars and three of his men would remain and begin preparations for a camp. They would build lean-tos and brush canopies to shelter the injured, and scout the area for water. The indications of abundant animal life pointed to probable nearby water sources.

David and his men began the return trip at once. It was much faster going down, even though they spent time checking the route to make certain it was the easiest way they could find. They broke out of the gorge into the Valley and were in sight of the camp by noon.

"David, there's something wrong. I feel it!" Eric said quietly.

"I sense something too, Eric. I'm glad we're back."

Alison was running toward Eric as she had before. But this time there was no joy in her face. She had been crying, and her face was lined with exhaustion. Eric felt a stab of fear. Ngambu—something had happened to Dr. Ngambu!

Alison fell exhausted into Eric's arms as they caught up to each other.

"Laurence—" she gasped. "Something has happened to Laurence. He just disappeared during the night, and we can't find any sign of him this morning!"

6 • Suspect Number One

Clearly the camp was disturbed by the disappearance of the young Frenchman. Michelle was crying hysterically. Alison's attempts to comfort her were unsuccessful. Captain McGuire and his crew were perplexed and frustrated.

"We've found nothing," said the Captain to David and Eric. "We woke up this morning and Mrs. Duchene began crying that her husband had disappeared. At first we thought it was nothing. We told her to look around—he had to be somewhere. But he wasn't. We helped her search farther from camp, and, finally, we made a systematic search for footprints leading into the desert. It's as if Laurence Duchene just vanished into thin air. It makes no sense whatever.

"But what of your climb? I take it you reached the top and left some of your men there."

David began relating the events of their ascent to the plateau. The Captain was grim-faced at the report of three more casualties. Eric left to rejoin Alison and Michelle. They were on the shady side of the fuselage by themselves. Sarah Lander was with them.

"Are there problems with anyone else?" Eric asked. "Dr. Ngambu—is he all right?"

Alison nodded.

Sarah reported, "He was up most of the night with his patients. I saw him about two this morning. I don't think he rested a minute after that."

"Did you notice Laurence at that time? I suppose he was lying somewhere near the doctor's pad."

"I didn't notice," Sarah confessed.

Eric turned to others.

"Did any of you notice him during the night?"

Alison shook her head.

"I didn't see or hear anything."

"I remember seeing Dr. Ngambu once or twice," said Michelle, "but that was all. I didn't notice whether Laurence was there at the time."

"Does he ever walk in his sleep?" Eric asked Michelle.

"I've never known him to."

"And no one else is missing from camp?"

"I checked on that," said Sarah. "Everybody is accounted for—except Laurence."

"I know it's been done already," said Eric, "but I've just got to make one more search for tracks leading away from camp. There's got to be some sign of the direction he took in leaving."

"But why would he go?" Michelle exclaimed. "There was no reason for him to leave!"

"We'll find the answer to that when we find Laurence. Let's go together—the four of us—out beyond the limits of the previous search. We'll circle the camp again for footprints leading away. We can't just say there aren't any. He didn't sprout wings and fly off."

The girls agreed. Michelle moved despondently, fearing that now, after Marie's death, Laurence was taken from her in some mysterious way.

Eric told Captain McGuire what they were going to do. He and David were completing plans for moving the camp.

"We've done it," said Captain McGuire. "But it will probably ease the girls' minds if you go over the ground once more. I have to admit I'm baffled. I see no explanation for that young fellow's disappearance."

"There has to be some answer."

"I hope you find it."

It was the hottest part of the day. The sun was bearing down from directly overhead, and the heat reflected from the east wall of the escarpment as from a stove. They moved along that wall, trying to distinguish from the many footprints of the exploring groups any that might belong to Laurence. It was a possibility that he might have gone either north or south along the wall, and his tracks would not stand out from those who had explored in those directions.

Eric spoke of this to the others.

"We'll have to hold that in the back of our minds. If we find nothing else, we may have to go in both directions along the wall to see if he went that way."

"But why would he—?" Michelle began. "I just don't believe it! It makes no sense that he would wander off in the middle of the night!"

They moved out a mile or so and then began to circle the camp, looking for tracks they might cross. There were none at this distance, except those along the wall. They moved slowly and carefully, not wanting to miss a single faint mark that might be Laurence's trail into the desert. The sun was lowering to the tops of the western cliffs when they reached a point on the opposite side of the airplane from which they had started.

"There's nothing here," said Michelle in tears. "There's just nothing."

Sarah frowned in deepening puzzlement.

"He was watching over Dr. Ngambu. Right? He was sleeping at right angles at the Doctor's head. Mary Hastings was a few feet beyond the Doctor, on the other side. And the Doctor was up with his patients from two o'clock on—"

"Eric!" Alison suddenly cried.

"What's the matter?"

"Look—if Laurence didn't go off into the desert during the night, then he must still be in the camp."

"Smart thinking," said Eric with a touch of sarcasm. "Just show us where."

"There! Nobody has looked for him there—"

Eric's eyes followed her pointing finger—to the broken airplane.

"You're crazy. If he's in the plane why doesn't he come out instead of playing cat and mouse with us?"

"Maybe he can't. Maybe he's tied. Maybe he's—" Alison looked at Michelle and stopped.

"Come on!" Eric broke into a run. The others followed.

There were plenty of compartments in the huge plane where something—or somebody—could be hidden. Baggage compartments. Passages under the floor where the control and fuel lines ran. The tail.

Eric grabbed Mr. Patterson and breathlessly explained their thinking. The flight engineer caught their urgency and led them to the plane. He forced open the twisted doors of baggage compartments not already opened, and they searched within. He led them inside the plane and opened the way to the compartments and passages under the floor of the cockpit and the cabin. He led them to the maintenance door in the tail.

The small compartment was an oven. Laurence was inside.

He was bound hand and foot and gagged. Eric grasped him by the shoulders and dragged him out to the floor. "Get Dr. Ngambu—quick!"

Alison ran in search of the Doctor.

Michelle threw herself upon Laurence, sobbing. "They've killed him! First Marie, and now Laurence—"

Eric pulled her away. "Michelle—we've got to help him. He may still be alive."

He slashed the cords on Laurence's hands and feet and tore the cloth from his mouth. He loosened the clothing and put his ear to his friend's chest.

"His heart's beating!" He grabbed a magazine cover from a torn seat. "Michelle—fan him with this. We'll get him out of here as soon as the Doctor comes."

Subduing her sobs, Michelle obeyed. As if in a nightmare, she waved the plastic cover before Laurence's face, stirring a breeze in the simmering air.

She searched his face for signs of life, but could see none.

Eric rubbed Laurence's wrists and ankles, which were swollen and blue from the pressure of the rope bindings. The flesh felt hot to his touch. It must have been close to 200 degrees in that metal compartment, Eric thought.

Alison appeared in the aisle, followed by Dr. Ngambu. She moved aside to let him pass. The Doctor exclaimed in dismay and knelt quickly beside Laurence. He checked with his stethoscope and examined the swollen wrists and ankles.

"Is he alive?" Michelle asked fearfully.

"Just barely. We must get him out of here quickly."

Mr. Patterson brought a stretcher. He and Eric got Laurence onto it and carried him out to the shade of the fuselage.

The crew who had gone for water from the spring had been successful in bringing back a good quantity. It was used now as Alison and Michelle sponged Laurence's face and body to draw out the burning heat. After a time, Dr. Ngambu administered a stimulant.

As the Doctor stepped back, Eric spoke quietly to him. "Does he have a chance?"

Dr. Ngambu nodded optimistically.

"A chance—yes. If only we had some oxygen—"

"There should be some in the plane's emergency respiratory system."

"Of course—I had forgotten. Could it be brought up if there is any?"

Mr. Patterson was doubtful, but he led the way with Eric to the tanks.

"I'm afraid they may have emptied themselves when the plane depressurized," he said. He checked the pressure gauge. "A little left. It may help."

They brought it alongside Laurence and attached a mask to allow a gentle flow of oxygen to pour over his face. It wouldn't last long.

"It is all we can do," said Dr. Ngambu at last.

They watched for the next hour. Laurence continued to lie as if dead. The rise and fall of his chest was barely detectable. His pulse remained faint and weak.

The sunlight faded, and the campfire was built up. An evening meal was prepared from the antelope meat. Spirits of the passengers were raised by the fresh nourishment, but were dampened again when word of the attack on Laurence was spread around.

Slowly, Laurence began to show signs of returning consciousness. His pulse grew stronger as his body finally cooled from the intense heat of his cramped prison. He opened his eyes and recognized Michelle. She took his hand and restrained herself from overwhelming him with her relief.

"Michelle—" his lips formed the word slowly, and he smiled at her.

After the meal, Sarah Lander rejoined the group.

"I think I understand what happened," she said. "The attackers were after Dr. Ngambu, but they knew Laurence had been planted as a guard, so they knew they must get him out of the way first. They crept up in the dark and clamped a chloroform cloth over his face. Then they dragged him quietly away and left him in the plane to die. They figured that was better than taking him out in the desert, where tracks could be followed.

They just didn't believe anyone would think of searching the plane."

"But they didn't attack the Doctor," said Eric.

"No. He got up right afterwards to care for some of the patients, and he didn't lie down again. By the time the attackers had bound and hidden Laurence in the plane, Dr. Ngambu was out of reach."

"But they haven't given up."

"No. They haven't given up," Sarah agreed.

"Maybe I could understand it if the Doctor were trying to hurt somebody," said Alison, "but all he's doing is helping. And he just happened to be on the same plane with all the rest of us when his enemies attacked the ship. So why should any of the other passengers want to kill him for that?"

"Don't try to look for any sense in this crazy world," Sarah responded. "That's just the way things are."

"It could be anybody," said Michelle in a thin, frightened voice. "We may never know who they are."

"You're right," said Eric. "We just might never find out who they are. But until we're rescued we've got to keep Dr. Ngambu from being hurt."

"Count me out right now!" Alison exploded angrily. "I'm sorry now we let you talk us into going along with your macho scheme. We failed, let's face it. The safety of the plane's passengers is Captain McGuire's responsibility. We've got to tell him what we know and what we suspect."

Eric smiled grimly.

"I've been trying to get up courage to do just that for the last hour. He's going to be plenty mad that we didn't let him know earlier. It might as well be now."

He got to his feet and started in the direction of the Captain who was seated with Mr. Patterson, in the shadows on the other side of the fire.

"Wait!" said Alison, already sorry that she had taken her fear out on her brother. "We're all going with you!"

Eric asked the two men to come with them to a spot where they wouldn't be overheard. They stood by the nose of the plane, at the edge of the firelight, and spoke in whispers.

"How's Laurence coming?" Captain McGuire asked. "It just doesn't make any sense. That insane attack on him!"

"He's coming around now," said Eric. "That's what we wanted to talk to you about, Sir."

Rapidly then, Eric told him of their plan to provide a second guard for Dr. Ngambu.

The Captain's face grew serious as he listened. "Why didn't you bring this to my attention at the time?"

"We realize now that we should have done so," said Eric miserably. "But we saw what pressure you were under taking care of all these people, and we thought we were helping by not loading you down with any more problems. We just wanted to help all we could."

"I certainly appreciate that. But your secretive efforts nearly cost Laurence his life."

"I am the one to blame, Captain McGuire. No one else," Eric admitted. "I wanted to keep the news from you, but only to help relieve you from one more problem."

"Well, Eric, I do need all the help I can get." McGuire smiled now. "I appreciate your eagerness to assume responsibility. But the important thing is to work together and keep in communication. O.K.?"

"We sure will," said Eric, relieved. The others nodded agreement.

"The problem is still a very serious one," the Captain went on. "Dr. Ngambu is probably the most valuable man in our whole group, at least along with David and Lars. We must protect him, not only for what he means to us as a doctor, but what he means to his nation. It appears as if he's *their* only hope.

"I'll assign Mr. Patterson to tighten up the surveillance over the Doctor and call you if he needs help. He'll recruit other members of the crew, who will be armed. And we must get Dr. Ngambu's cooperation. He may not be adequately concerned about his own danger."

"I'm sure he's well aware of it," said Sarah. "He's just not going to let it interfere with his medical duties. You see, he has a kind of belief that he *is* responsible for the disaster to the plane and all these people. He feels he really owes them his life for what he has caused, that he has to make it up to them somehow for this thing."

"I can understand that," said the Captain. "That's exactly the kind of man he is.

"There's one thing I would like you to do, Eric. Keep an eye on old Jakob Vroorman. He's started to get up and move around in spite of the Doctor's warning not to."

"Why do you think he needs watching?" asked Eric.

"He hates Dr. Ngambu. Remember?"

"You don't think he—?" exclaimed Alison.

"I don't think anything," Captain McGuire said. "I just want you to observe and report to me anything out of the ordinary. I've noticed him talking with several of the other passengers in a kind of secretive way. I just don't know. A man that hates the Doctor as much as Vroorman does cannot be ignored."

"I see what you mean," said Eric. "While he's too injured to do anything himself, he might influence others."

"It's just barely possible—and I don't want to overlook any possibilities. Now, you take care of Laurence tonight. I'll see that Mr. Patterson sets a watch on the Doctor."

"Thank you," said Alison. "I'm glad you're not really mad at us, Captain."

McGuire smiled again.

"I wish we had more people here who are as willing to help as much as you are."

Laurence struggled to remain conscious during the early part of the night. Michelle sat by his side and spoke to him as he stirred, but he lay quietly without any movement for long periods of time.

Alison and Eric took turns sleeping and watching. They tried to get Michelle to sleep a little, too, but she refused. Sarah sat with them, sometimes dozing, sometimes awake and watching, scanning the camp for suspicious movements.

When Alison got up to take her turn on watch, she bent down to put her blanket over Sarah sleeping next to her. Immediately Alison was facing the barrel of an automatic pistol in Sarah's hand.

7 • *Secret Attack*

"It's absolutely none of your business, Eric, why I keep a loaded gun. I've got a right to protect myself from the thugs that seem to have crawled aboard that plane," Sarah snapped. "But I'm sorry to have scared Alison. When she put her blanket over me, it awakened me. I responded intuitively.

"It wouldn't be the first time, either," Sarah explained. "I've got permission to carry it in at least twenty countries. Don't worry about having to report it to the Captain. He knows I have it!"

Eric had learned about the weapon from the shaken Alison. He was through keeping secrets from the captain, even though he was sure the gentleman would not like to hear about this new development.

Eric wondered just how much the toughtalking Sarah Lander was for real. He had seen her as sympathetic as a mother to those who were hurt and exhausted. He had heard her talk as tough as a dockworker to those she considered to be out of line.

"I'll bet you're a regular Annie Oakley," he said soothingly.

"You might be very surprised. My college had a women's shooting team. I was captain for two years."

The move to the plateau began the next morning. David took charge of the people who were the most ablebodied of the passengers. At least a fourth of these would be needed to return, after they had gained experience on the trail, to help the weak and injured the following day. Eric, Ralph Botts, and the two Africans, John Mrak and Ald Jamez, were each assigned a group of twenty to lead up through the gorge. Mary Hastings was included to prepare facilities on the plateau to care for the injured, who would be coming up later.

Each passenger was allowed to take what personal possessions he could carry in a small overnight bag or an airline bag. Some wanted to drag along large suitcases and had to be persuaded they could not do this. Eric took his briefcase with only his valuable research papers and a few items of clothing.

They started early, before the day heated up. Most of the survivors had lost track of time, but according to the careful entries in Alison's journal, it was their fifth day in the Valley of Death.

The heat and exertion of the climb was difficult. Yet the majority of them reached the top by late afternoon.

The ascent went far better than Eric had imagined it could possibly go. Perhaps the smell of smoke and roasting meat gave them courage for the final steep ascent to the plateau.

David and Lars greeted each other with laughter and back slapping like longlost brothers.

"I thought you were never going to get here," laughed Lars. "What took you so long?"

"I knew you wouldn't have anything ready," teased David. "Where are the huts you were going to build? Where's the big dinner that's supposed to be waiting for us?"

"There." Lars pointed to a makeshift spit where several quarters of antelope were browning. He didn't say that the lions got a good part of it. Or that they heard baboons during the night. It was pretty wild country to which they had come for survival.

Instead, he said, "Good news! We've found a spring of fresh water about a half mile away."

"That is good news. So—get things started. These folks are hungry and will welcome a place to bed down for the night. Eric and I will take the training group back down as soon as we eat. We'll bring up the second batch tomorrow."

"We'll give these folks our first-class accommodations," Lars said with modest hospitality.

Just as darkness set in they reached the camp. It was important to be off the trail and back in camp by sunset. David and Eric reported immediately to Captain McGuire, who was pleased to know that the descent had gone so well.

The evening fire was going, and a fresh antelope quarter that Eric and David had brought down was cut into small steaks and roasts to hang over the fire. There was almost a party spirit in the air.

Eric sought out Alison and their friends. "Anything

going on today?'' he said. "How is Laurence coming?"

"I'm doing fine—for one well-roasted Frenchman."

The girls stepped aside and Eric saw Laurence Duchene sitting up on the sand behind them.

"Isn't he looking fine!" Michelle beamed and leaned down to give her husband a hug.

Eric shared her feelings, nodding his agreement. He hadn't expected Duchene to be so well recovered. Eric sat down casually beside Laurence.

"You're looking great! Do you feel like telling me what happened?"

Laurence laughed.

"I could have told it a hundred times today—if there was anything to tell. Unfortunately, there isn't. I just don't remember a thing except the sudden clamping of a chloroform cloth over my face and being seized by the arms and legs. The next thing I knew I became half conscious in that hot box they tell me was in the tail of the airplane. I hadn't the faintest idea of where I was. All I knew was that I could hardly breathe. I believed I was going to die. I don't remember anything more until this morning."

"I'm so sorry," said Eric humbly. "If I hadn't tried to talk everybody into taking the responsibility of guarding Dr. Ngambu it wouldn't have happened. I almost cost you your life."

Laurence touched his arm.

"Don't blame yourself, Eric. You couldn't know what was going to happen. It's not your fault."

Eric had trouble with his voice choking up on him. Finally, he said, "You got no clue as to who your attackers were?"

"No. I didn't see them or hear them. Just nothing."
Laurence seemed to suffer a chill for a moment.
"So—" he said, "they're still watching—still
waiting—"

"But we've got help now. Mr. Patterson has beefed
up protection for the Doctor."

Laurence nodded.

"But the attackers are still free. They'll try again to
get Dr. Ngambu—and anyone who stands between him
and them. That includes you and me, Sarah, the
girls—"

Eric could understand his friend's fear. It would take
Laurence a long time to forget that ordeal.

"Do you feel strong enough to get up?" asked Eric.

"I've been walking around this afternoon. Feel almost normal."

"Perhaps it would be a good idea for you and the
girls to go up to the plateau with the group tomorrow.
Provided the Captain agrees." Eric turned to his sister.
"They need your kind of help up there, Alison."

"Sure, I can make it. I have a free day," Alison
answered saucily. He hadn't seen that kind of spirit
in his twin since the crash.

Captain McGuire agreed to Eric's proposal. He questioned David and Eric about the facilities on top.

"I think we should send the most seriously injured
tomorrow," he said finally. "Dr. Ngambu says they are
fading rapidly in this heat. Two more died today."
David agreed.

"Dr. Ngambu can come with that group. We'll send
back some ablebodied men to help the least injured—
those who can walk—the following day. The rest of you

can come then. That will complete the move."

Eric lay down that night thinking of the enormous tasks they would have getting the stretcher cases up the gorge. Some would die on the way, he was sure of that. But more would die if they stayed.

He had spotted the contrails from two high-flying planes on the regular run from Nairobi to Tel Aviv. The planes themselves were too high to be seen, and their crews could not possibly have seen the tiny spot of wreckage in the Valley. Eric had stopped looking for rescue planes.

Nearby, Alison squirmed on the hard sand. "Aren't you sleeping?" she asked.

"Sure," he laughed softly. "How about you?"

"Eric—do you think we'll ever be found. I try to keep up my spirits around people, but inside I'm scared. How long can we live like this?"

"A long time, Sis. There's plenty of meat above. There's a spring of good water. I guess the big thing is ammunition for hunting. I don't know how much David and Lars have."

"But in the end it will be gone—"

"Unless we are found. And I don't know when that will be—if ever. What I've been thinking the last couple of days is that after we get settled up there, the Captain will probably send an expedition on foot toward Nairobi. David, Lars, and Mary Hastings—and maybe some others I don't know about—all have enough African experience for such an expedition. I don't know what the risks would be, but I'll bet that right now David and Lars and Mary have the same idea going through their heads."

"I hope so. We've had our share of aborted missions. Good night, Eric. I think you're great!"

For several hours Eric stayed awake, trying to rid himself of the doubts that continued to haunt him. How long could they really survive on the plateau? Could an expedition to Nairobi really succeed?

Whatever the risks, he felt that a party must be sent in the direction of Nairobi as quickly as possible. Like tomorrow. Silently he prayed for help. Finally he slept.

In the morning the second group was assembled by firelight, even before the faintest hint of dawn. The twenty serious stretcher cases were readied for the arduous trip. Dr. Ngambu did everything he could to prepare them. Some, it seemed certain, would not survive the journey. But neither would they survive their sixth day in the heat of the Valley floor.

As he neared the completion of his preparations, the Doctor approached Eric.

"I would like you to do something special for me—you and your friends," he said.

"Of course. Anything—"

"I want you to escort Jakob Vroorman and take care of him on the way. Under no circumstances should he attempt to make such a climb as this, but he refuses all my advice, as you well know. I can do nothing more for him. Please look after him, if you can."

Eric looked at him in astonishment.

"Why should you be especially concerned about him? Of all the people here, he—"

Dr. Ngambu smiled faintly and held up his hand.

"I know. I know, Eric. He hates that 'nigger doctor' he's been forced to submit to, and I really have enough to see to without trying to change him, when there are so many others who need me.''

"Right! If he hasn't got sense enough to let himself be carried on a stretcher—''

"I am as responsible for his condition as I am for any of the others. I have to do all I can." Dr. Ngambu's voice was near pleading now. "If you will help me, Eric—''

Eric felt suddenly ashamed of his own animosity toward Jakob Vroorman. "Of course," he said finally. "Of course I'll do everything I can to help.''

"Thank you. That eases my mind considerably.''

Eric watched him walk away—and then thought of Captain McGuire's caution about Jakob Vroorman. The Captain had asked them to watch him for possible implication in attacks against Dr. Ngambu. And now the Doctor was asking them to help him save the Afrikaner from his own stubbornness and foolishness. Eric shook his head. He thought he knew what it meant to be a Christian. But he wasn't sure that he had seen Christlike love in action—until he met Dr. Ngambu.

He told Alison and the Duchenes about the Doctor's special request that he look out for Jakob Vroorman. They were as amazed as Eric by the Doctor's completely selfless attitude. How could he be so concerned about Jakob Vroorman, who openly hated him?

Eric walked slowly toward the spot where the old Afrikaner was struggling to get himself ready for the journey. Was it possible that the old man might be involved in possible attacks on the Doctor? It seemed unlikely, Eric thought. True enough, Vroorman hated the Doctor, but his reasons and his feelings were different from those of the fanatics who considered the Doctor a Jonah who had to be destroyed because he had brought disaster upon them. Eric found it hard to believe Vroorman had any connection with the attackers.

But the Captain's feelings could not be ignored, either.

Eric approached as Jakob Vroorman got to his feet, adjusting his clothes. His mane of white hair spread wildly in all directions. His cheeks were hollow and pale in spite of the deep tan of his skin. He was still wearing his bloodstained undershirt.

"Good morning," said Eric. "How do you feel?"

The old man glared at him from beneath shaggy, white eyebrows. His jaws worked a moment before he answered, as if he wanted to spit out something first.

"I feel like I've had my stomach ripped open and a hot iron rammed inside me. That's what I feel like. Anything else you want to know?"

"I'm guiding the section of the group you're in," said Eric. "It's my responsibility to help make sure everybody gets to the top OK."

"Whether I make it or not is nobody's responsibility but my own," said Jakob Vroorman. "You take care of yourself, young fellow, and I'll take care of old Jakob Vroorman. Is that fair enough?"

"It certainly is, but if you have any trouble making it, I want to give you a hand. I've been up and back twice now, and I know the way pretty well."

"Then you won't have any trouble finding your way."

102

"You can follow me closely and I'll help you over the rough spots. There are some pretty bad ones."

"Jakob Vroorman never followed anybody. And I've been over rougher spots than you'll ever see. Go give your help to somebody who needs it. I don't!"

Eric held back the anger that rose inside him. He smiled and tried to keep his voice calm.

"I'll be watching, anyway, Mr. Vroorman," he said with a forced smile. "If you need anything, I won't be far."

The old man made no answer as Eric moved away. Eric remembered Mary Hasting's words when she spoke of knowing Vroorman years ago: "He was impossible then and he hasn't improved any with age."

She was so right!

They moved out an hour earlier than the previous day's groups. They also moved much more slowly. The stretcher-bearers were selected from the uninjured men among the passengers. Fortunately, there were enough of them to carry the awkward burdens and to spell each other off so there were rest periods for each one.

Two bearers carried each patient. For several heavier ones, four were used. Except for those from the plane's emergency equipment, hastily constructed stretchers were awkward and unsteady. They had been assembled from scrap metal tubing and rough branches collected on earlier climbs to the plateau. These had been covered with fabric from inside the plane with pieces of metal cable substituting for pins. Eric knew some of them would need repair before they reached the top, so he collected a few spare bits of metal and fabric and carried them with the briefcase in his backpack.

As the long line trudged slowly toward the gorge in the dim morning light, Dr. Ngambu, despite his exhausting efforts of the past days, moved continually among his patients, checking, comforting, administering painkillers where necessary.

"I don't see how he does it," said Alison. "He has enough energy for ten of the rest of us."

In addition to Mr. Patterson's watch over the Doctor, Sarah Lander remained close, never taking her eyes from him, following all his movements among his patients. Somehow she always kept between him and others who walked nearby, yet she stayed out of his way, so that he scarcely was aware of her presence.

Alison whispered to Eric, "Sarah's got the idea that if another attempt is going to be made against Dr. Ngambu it will happen on the trail."

"She could be right. But Patterson and two of his stewards are watching, too. It would be hard for anything to happen here with all that guarding."

"Let's hope so. For anything to happen to him would be the worst tragedy of this whole thing."

The long line came finally to the entrance of the gorge. When some of the injured saw the rugged slopes ahead they groaned in disbelief.

"It's an impossibility!" one of the strongest bearers groaned.

"Did I stay alive this long to fall to my death?" a woman shrieked.

David urged them on, promising it could be done.

Laurence was already exhausted. He leaned against a rock, breathing painfully. He looked up to the path ahead and shook his head in dismay. "I guess I'm not as much recovered as I thought. I'm not sure I can make it, Eric.''

Eric threw an arm about his friend's shoulder.

"If you can't we'll carry you. But that old man over there is making it. If he can, so can you.''

Laurence glanced toward Jakob Vroorman, resting from his own exhaustion fifty feet away.

"No matter how quarrelsome he is, you can't help admiring him. He's—what do you Americans say?— He's—got guts.''

"He has that, for sure. I wonder what else there is in him that makes him tick. I suppose nobody will ever know.''

The old Afrikaner slumped heavily against the rock, and for a moment Eric thought he had fainted. Then Vroorman straightened and seemed to look right at them. He grinned defiantly as if to say there was nothing old Jakob Vroorman couldn't lick—or at least die trying.

"Tough old bird!'' Eric whispered under his breath.

Laurence touched his arm.

"Seriously—if somehow I shouldn't make it through, will you promise that you and Alison will look after Michelle and help her get back to Paris?''

"Come on—there's no need of thoughts like that!''

"Will you promise me?''

"I promise.''

They began the climb.

Almost immediately, one of the stretcher-bearers stumbled. Another man grabbed the stretcher, but the patient was jolted harshly. They moved on.

When the first hundred feet of altitude were reached,

they could look back to the Valley floor with a small sense of accomplishment. It lifted their spirits.

By midmorning the sun was over them. Its rays burned down in merciless intensity. In the Valley, the shade of the airplane had been some protection, but now even that was missing. And Eric noted they were only a quarter as far along the trail as the other parties had been at this time—in spite of their early start. At this rate they would not be off the trail by the time it was dark.

An abundance of water was brought along and was distributed liberally, but this only partially offset the effects of the heat. The line paused for a few minutes every fifteen minutes. And at noon they rested an hour while they ate a meal of cold antelope meat prepared the day before. There was a general groan when they were called to resume the climb.

"How fast do we have to go to reach the top by dark?" Eric asked David.

"A lot faster. I hate to do it, but I'll have to shorten the rest stops."

Exhaustion was spreading like an epidemic.

Eric kept his eye on Jakob Vroorman, who obviously wanted no help from anyone. Pain showed in his face and eyes as he fought to keep pace with the aid only of a thick wooden staff one of the crewmen had cut for him before they had left the plane. With great effort, however, he kept up with the climbers.

Laurence was having great trouble. He was forced to lean heavily on Michelle, as much as he disliked burdening her. The imprisonment in the oven-like tail of the plane had left him more weakened than he had thought. Alison and Eric took turns with Michelle in giving Laurence support.

Sarah Lander dropped back to talk with them, still keeping an eye on Dr. Ngambu as he shuttled back and forth among his patients.

"There's a lot of grumbling up ahead," said Sarah. "I can't understand most of it. Some of the people seem to be saying they've just been brought up here to die. But most of the talk I think is about Dr. Ngambu. They're saying again—in some pretty violent language, as near as I can gather—that everything is all his fault and he ought to be made to pay."

"David should know what's going on, if he doesn't already."

"I've told Patterson. He's hearing some of it, too. He'll let David know. I'm wondering if they're trying to stir up a mass attack on the Doctor right here on the trail. A couple of dozen of them could have things their own way if they decided to—"

"Look—!" Alison suddenly pointed ahead and exclaimed in a whisper. "That man—he's deliberately working his way toward the Doctor. I've been watching him—"

Sarah nodded in sudden urgency.

"I noticed him, too. I've got to get up there!"

The man was now behind and to the left of Dr. Ngambu. Suddenly he stumbled and lunged forward. Sarah stiffened, and her automatic appeared in her hand. She leveled it toward the falling figure and three rapid shots burst from her gun.

8 • A New Threat

The falling man twisted and careened over the edge of the precipice. His outflung arm struck Dr. Ngambu, who struggled for balance and slid over the edge.

Screams filled the air as the shots thundered against the walls of the gorge. Cries of alarm and rage erupted in several languages. All eyes were on Sarah in terrible fascination as she stood with the gun still in her hand. Her wild mane of hair stirred in the faint waft of air.

Then they slowly peered over the slope.

Dr. Ngambu was lying on a narrow ledge twenty feet below. The other man had fallen all the way to the bottom of the gorge.

David pushed his way through the group. "What happened?" he demanded.

Sarah spoke calmly. "A man tried to shove Dr. Ngambu over the edge by pretending to stumble against him. I shot the attacker. But I may not have saved the Doctor, after all."

Patterson was already being lowered over the edge on a nylon line by two of the stewards and a couple of other men.

"Get back!" David ordered as the crowd pressed forward to see the Doctor. "We don't want any more over the edge."

Eric saw the flight engineer reach Dr. Ngambu and bend over to listen to his chest. Patterson waved back, and in a moment the Doctor struggled to sit up, with Patterson's support. Suddenly he smiled and waved a hand weakly to those above.

A rope sling was quickly fashioned, and the Doctor was drawn up. He sat for a moment while the ropes were removed. Then he spotted Sarah. "Thank you," he said.

"Thank you, my dear. You certainly saved my life."

David knelt beside him.

"What happened?"

"I saw a man out of the corner of my eye fake a stumble and try to shove me over. I tried to dodge him, but I wasn't fast enough. Sarah came to my rescue. The force of his push was reduced, but his own momentum sent him over the edge."

David straightened up and faced Sarah.

"You saved a good man's life."

Sarah turned to the onlookers, who clustered in small groups along the trail, some fearful, some angry and enraged, a few seemingly unconcerned. The friends of the dead man were sullen with rage. Her face was pale and hard.

"I think it's time we got this little matter straightened out," she said in a brittle voice. "If any of the rest of you have any queer ideas about getting even with Dr. Ngambu because you have the crazy notion he's responsible for the mess we're in, I'm serving notice now that I'll personally take you on one at a time or all together. This madness stops *now*!"

She let the automatic pistol lie idly in her hand so all could see it.

"Have you all got that?" She looked around, fixing each one in the eye. Some glared back at her in fury. Others turned away.

"One at a time, or all together." Her words were slow and spaced in the silence that surrounded them. "You'd better have it real good. Or you can expect the same as he got." She gestured over the precipice.

Dr. Ngambu was able to walk. He had landed on his left shoulder at the bottom of the slope. He was badly bruised, but he had no broken bones. When he recovered his wind, he felt his strength returning. Only the shoulder pained him.

The climb resumed. Spirits were numbed by the shock of the attack on the Doctor and Sarah's shooting of his assailant. There was little conversation. Everyone seemed willing to move faster, as if wanting to put as much distance as possible between them and the scene of tragedy on the trail.

As they moved, Jakob Vroorman plodded forward, jabbing his stout staff rapidly on the trail to catch up to Sarah. She whirled defensively at his touch on her arm from behind.

"It's just me," he said, grinning through his pain. "I just wanted to say you made a great show. You're tough, Miss. Stay in Africa and make a piece of it

110

yours. Only the tough ones make it out here."

Her face softened. She smiled gently at the genuine admiration in his eyes.

"Thanks, Mr. Vroorman. I appreciate your kind words. I don't know if I'm tough or not. I just try to do what has to be done."

"You're all right, Miss. You're just all right." He waved his hand to her and let the line pass him by.

The last few hundred feet of the climb were agony. It was dark. A few flashlights provided feeble circles of light, but they didn't prevent people from falling. David and Eric and the other leaders guided them carefully. Many were sobbing in exhaustion. The stretcher-bearers and their burdens were almost beyond their endurance.

At last they came to a place where the yellow glow of firelight could be seen beyond the edge of the precipice. One by one, and two by two, they climbed slowly over the edge. David gave them each a hand over the final step.

Some threw themselves flat on the ground in exhaustion. Some began to laugh hysterically, as if they never believed they would make it. Eric waited to the end of the line to give Laurence a hand. He was leaning on Michelle and Alison. The last person, a hundred feet behind all the others, was Jakob Vroorman. He was forced to take Eric's hand to be helped up the last step.

Mary Hastings was waiting. She had directed the construction of a long, rough covering made from acacia branches to shelter the patients. The stretchers were laid beneath it, and she began at once to attend to them.

"What happened to you?" she exclaimed as Dr. Ngambu approached with his bloody shirt and injured shoulder. "Here, let me take care of that shoulder!"

He waved her away.

"No. I'm all right, Mary. Let's see to our patients."

Sadly, they found that two more had died quietly and without anyone's awareness during the final hours of the climb.

Dr. Ngambu shook his head.

"I should have been able to do more for them. I should have done more—"

"You won't be able to do anything at all if you don't let me take care of that shoulder," Mary scolded.

Meat and water had been prepared by Lars and his crew. Grass pads had been made for sleeping—an unbelievable luxury after the hard sand of the Valley below. The air seemed far cooler, too.

Eric and Alison joined their friends in the meal of antelope roast.

"This seems like a paradise up here, compared with the Valley," Alison commented between bites of roasted meat.

Laurence was lying nearby on a grass pad where Michelle was encouraging him to eat.

"It may seem like paradise," he said, "unless we have to stay here forever."

"One day at a time," said Eric. "We're better off today than yesterday. Tomorrow—better still."

Laurence struggled to a sitting position.

"But they're not going to find us now, are they? They aren't sending any rescue planes over. What else is there for us?"

"Through the jungle—some of us—on foot," said Eric. "I'm sure it will come to that. It must be five or six hundred miles to Nairobi. But there are villages closer than that, from which messages could be sent. I think that's the way it will have to be."

"That would take weeks!" exclaimed Michelle.

"Six to eight, maybe. Anybody got a better answer?"

They fell silent. Their meal over, they lay down on the grass pads and quickly dropped into the sleep of exhaustion.

Early the next morning, Eric joined David and a dozen others as they started back to bring up the remaining group in the camp. On their way down they were surprised to see Captain McGuire and the remaining group of people assembled in the gorge.

When they reached him, Captain McGuire explained, "We decided we could save some time by meeting you here, since we knew you'd be down this morning."

David was not entirely pleased. "We might not have made it by this time, Captain."

"Then we might have started up without you. We lost two more people last night. They weren't the most seriously hurt, either. The heat exhaustion simply finished them off. We had no choice. One more day in the Valley would have been the end of most of us."

"I understand. Let's get moving. We'll help you with the stretchers and the water."

The Captain himself had almost reached the end of his endurance. The pain of his head wounds, which had received little attention, combined with the intense heat to drain his resources to the limit. With the other injured who were able to walk, he made the climb with extreme difficulty, requiring assistance during a good part of the way.

Just at the edge of darkness, the final party reached the plateau. They were welcomed and made comfortable for the night.

Eric decided now to approach David about the question of what they would do next. He caught David alone, eating a chunk of antelope roast in the shadows beyond the firelight.

The naturalist smiled and held out a chunk of meat. "Not bad. Have some."

"I've had mine. Thanks."

"I think tonight ought to be a celebration. To tell you the truth, I wasn't sure until now that we'd succeed in getting everybody out of the Valley. I don't ever want to try anything like that again."

"Me, either," said Eric. "But we're not out of the woods yet. What happens next?"

David looked at him seriously. "What do you think ought to happen next?"

"It looks as if the air search—if any—is so far off the track that they'll never find us. So we can forget about it. I think the next move is up to us, on foot. To Nairobi."

"That's what Lars and I have been considering for the past several days."

"Then it's settled?"

"Yes. But there's one other person I'd like to ask about it. Mary Hastings knows more about this part of Africa than anybody else here. Let's put it to her."

He signaled to the missionary nurse, who was moving

among the seriously hurt patients under the shelter nearby.

"Mary, what do you think about making a trek through the jungle from here to Nairobi?" David asked.

She looked at him and Eric seriously.

"You've given up on an air rescue?"

"I think we have to," David replied.

"Do you know where we are?" she asked.

David looked puzzled.

"On the edge of the Great Rift, about five or six hundred miles from Nairobi."

"That isn't what I meant. We're in the depths of Turnabo country."

It was Eric's turn to look puzzled. "I don't understand what you're talking about."

"The Turnabo," said Mary, "are probably the last of the savage primitive peoples of Africa. They are a nomadic tribe and appear unexpectedly whenever they receive word of food supplies for their cattle or themselves. The chance of a small party getting through their territory without capture and certain death is almost zero."

"Well—how safe are we right here?"

"Not very. But we're a bigger group. We have a somewhat better chance of palavering with them if they challenge us. I have known some of their chiefs in times past. Even made friends with two of them. They may remember me. We stand some chance, at least, while we're here together. A few of us trying to cross their country would stand almost no chance."

"So you think that's completely out?" said David.

"I suppose in the end we might want to try a run through the Turnabo country rather than starving to death after our ammunition runs out. But I don't think it's a wise decision until we're forced to it. I'm still hoping we'll be spotted from the air."

Mary returned to her care of the wounded. David and Eric looked at each other in silence.

"It still may be the only way," David said finally, "in spite of Mary's warning. We'll have to kick it around with McGuire when he's had a rest and see how he feels concerning the risks. In the meantime, the question is, how long do we wait?"

"How much ammunition do you have?" Eric asked.

"There's enough to last a long time—if we don't have to waste it on lions and baboons attacking the camp."

The very sound of those words was unpleasant. Everything seemed to rest between a decision as to how long to wait for air rescue—which seemed hopeless—or whether an overland trek was worth the risk.

"And one other thing," David added. "We've got people dying for lack of medical help and treatment."

Most of the camp had settled down by the time Eric lay on his grass pad. Alison was awake and he told her what David and Mary had said. She sat up excitedly. "But surely Mary could help! If she could locate some of her old chief acquaintances among the nearby tribesmen, I'll bet she could negotiate with them for guides to take our party through their country."

"It's an idea. I wonder why Mary didn't think of it. We'll have to see what she says about it."

They lay back on their grass pads listening to the

night sounds of the jungle. Eric stared up at the stars and reviewed possible plans for a trek to Nairobi. Even after all the intense effort of the past few days he found himself unable to sleep. He heard his companions stirring and guessed they couldn't either. Alison squirmed and faced him from a few feet away.

"You asleep?" she whispered.

"Sure. Completely dead to the world. What's on your mind?"

"I wonder what's going on back home. Do you ever wonder?"

"I think about it. Central High is probably gearing up for fall football practice and hoping they can come up with a team that can beat Riverside this year."

Alison laughed faintly.

"I'll bet Aunt Rose is in the garden right now, fussing over the chrysanthemums she hopes will bloom before anyone else's in town this summer."

"What I wonder most of all," said Eric, "is what Dad is doing down in Capetown. He must be driving everybody in the institute, the government, and the airline crazy trying to find out what happened to our plane."

"I wouldn't be surprised if he's flown up to Nairobi and is there right now chewing on everybody. He must be working up a real storm—" Suddenly Alison was still. "What was that?"

"What was what?" said Eric. "I didn't hear anything."

"Not hear. Feel. I felt something. Like a drum beating in the earth—not a sound, but a feeling."

"Oh, Sis—!"

"There! There it is again."

Eric lay very still. Beneath him, a low rumble and throbbing seemed to come up from the earth itself.

"Eric—it's an earthquake!" Alison's voice was the whispered scream of a very frightened girl.

"Sis—quiet!" Eric whispered intensely. "Don't scare everybody."

"I'm sorry. Maybe I'm just jittery." Her voice quieted, but she seemed on the verge of tears. "I'm so scared, Eric!"

"Take it easy, Sis." Eric moved his pad to be closer. "Whatever happens, God promised to help us through it—for as long as we're in this old world."

"But I've had enough!" Her shoulders began to shake with her sobs.

"So who hasn't!" Eric held her tightly in his arms until he felt her relax.

Within seconds Alison's tearstained face looked with a faint smile into Eric's. The velvet brown eyes sparkled for the moment.

"You're so right, Twinny. I know the Lord promised He would be with us—even through the end of the world. It's—well, it's just not knowing what's next maybe. I want to know so we can be prepared to handle it."

"Maybe God knew we would try to handle it all ourselves—and mess everything up even worse for everybody involved—if we knew what's ahead. Seems to me I remember His telling us just to trust Him—to count on Him, no matter what."

Alison nodded. "That's probably what the motto on Gramps' desk means—the one that says, 'Trust in the Lord with all your heart and lean not on your own understanding. In all your ways—"

Suddenly her body stiffened and trembled.

"There it is again."

There was no mistaking it this time. The earth growled and shook beneath them.

"I smell sulfur."

The odor of rotten egg gas reminded Eric of their high school chemistry lab, where the biggest joke of the year was to generate sulfur dioxide gas in some unsuspecting English teacher's room.

He turned to look around behind them, and then he exclaimed in sudden awe and fear, "Oh—!"

Alison and the others near them turned and gasped aloud. The big mountain about twenty miles east of their camp had a thin crescent of light at its tip, and a dim glow spread into the sky. Eric remembered his uneasiness the first time he had seen the mountain, with its telltale cone.

"The volcano! There's lava inside lighting up the rim!"

"Is it going to erupt?" Michelle questioned in a worried tone.

"There's no way of telling," Eric replied. "Doesn't look like it erupted around here recently. It probably just simmers and rumbles without erupting." He heard himself speaking, but didn't believe what he was saying.

More to calm the others than anything else, he lay down. He stayed awake, listening to the rumble, and feeling it in the earth beneath him. He knew little about volcanoes. The only thing he was sure of was that no one could run fast enough or far enough to escape the outpouring from an eruption. And there was no way the weakened and injured could run anywhere.

"If ever there is a time, Alison, to count on God—no matter what—this is it!"

Alison's eyes were swimming in frightened tears, but her nod told Eric she agreed. "It's just those God given 'self-protective fear responses'—as Dad calls them—that get me so uptight."

"Guess we'd better be glad for the way God's made our bodies to respond to possible danger. It's for our own protection."

Eric began, "Lord, we really want to trust You, especially when we feel so scared. We know You're here with us—whether we feel like it or not—'cause You said You would never leave us. Thanks for reminding us. Thanks a whole lot, Father."

"Amen!" Alison agreed.

The jungle creatures had been roused by the volcanic disturbance. Eric could identify the roar of lions, the screeches of monkeys, the howls of baboons among the many night noises around them. It was as if the whole animal kingdom was singing some song of primitive fear in response to the ominous thunder of the volcano.

Eric continued to feel jittery. So did everyone else. The buzz of fearful conversation was punctuated by occasional wailings. Someone threw more wood on the dying embers of the campfire.

David was moving about on the far edge of the light, gun in hand, on guard against frightened animals that might invade or stampede the camp. Patterson and the stewards were standing guard near Dr. Ngambu sleeping fitfully at one end of the shelters. Sarah was not far away, her gun ready.

The threat of the volcano was something new. Up to now there had only been the heat and injuries and food and the threat to the Doctor's life to worry about. Now—

Eric heard the shrill talk in the dark beyond the fire. He caught phrases of French, Italian, and frequent comments in English. Some were complaining bitterly that they should never have left the Valley floor. They were at least safe down there by the plane. Someone would have spotted it and come to take them to safety. Now they would die in the eruption of a volcano.

Just like the children of Israel, Eric thought, all the time crying and complaining to Moses that they were going to die in the desert—crying to return to Egypt and blaming him for ever having led them out of their slavery.

Eric got up and looked around for David. He found the naturalist with Mary and Captain McGuire. They were already discussing the new threat.

David was saying, "There's no question of moving away from it. There's no way we can move fast enough to be out of its reach if it blows."

"Is there anything at all that we can do to protect ourselves in case that happens?" McGuire asked.

"These volcanoes in the Rift Valley occasionally blow out clouds of suffocating soda ash. Have everybody tear up some cloth—shirts, dresses, whatever— and have some water nearby to use for dampened breathing masks. Tomorrow, let's build more acacia branch shelters and make them as tight as possible against falling soda ash."

"What about lava flow?"

"It could happen. But it's not likely to be great enough to be a threat. All we can do is hope this one runs true to form."

While they stood discussing their plans, a group of nearly a dozen passengers began moving toward the camp leaders. They approached shaking their fists and shouting as they came. Their words were an angry mix of French, Italian, and African languages.

The leader was a huge African wearing a turban.

Shaking his fist in Captain McGuire's face, he screamed, "We're going back down! Everybody will die up here under the volcano. You brought us up here to die!"

"Go back, then," said McGuire quietly. "No one is forcing you to stay. I suggest you wait until daylight, however."

"We will go now!"

"Suit yourselves. I'd also like to remind you that if the volcano blows, there will be just as much soda ash pouring down on the camp in the Valley as there will be up here."

That stopped them for a moment. They turned and consulted with each other. A couple turned away and went back to their pads. But the leader swung around and glared savagely at the Captain. "You lie to get us killed! We're going down!"

Ten men traveled to the edge of the plateau where the trail to the Valley began. The leader lowered himself over the edge into the blackness. The others followed.

David watched them sadly.

"They'll never make it down alive."

Captain McGuire rubbed a hand across his tired face.

"I have done all I can for them. I'm afraid their own stupidity is going to kill them."

"There's nothing more we can do now." David commented wearily. "Let's get some sleep. In the morning we'll get going on the shelters and alert the people about preparing wet masks."

Work was begun as soon as breakfast was completed the following morning to increase the expanse of sheltered area. To Eric it seemed like futile effort. Flimsy overhead structures such as these could do little to hold back a rain of volcanic ash and dust. But it was something to do. It allowed the passengers to put their minds on something besides their seemingly hopeless situation.

Dr. Ngambu had his arm bound in a sling close to his body, and went about his rounds among the injured with a tender concern for each one. Sarah followed him openly now, her gun plainly visible, never more than a few feet away. The Doctor protested her hovering over him so diligently, but she ignored his protests with a smile and continued her watch. It amused her to see the look of rage in the eyes of some who watched her gun as she moved above. She was sure that those who had tried to kill Laurence and who wanted to murder the Doctor were still among them. If she only knew which ones—

Jakob Vroorman kept to himself as usual, never making a sound of protest against the pain and exhaustion within him. His large wound had broken open again during the climb. He said nothing about it until

Mary Hastings discovered it during her rounds. He had to submit to her stitching it up again under Dr. Ngambu's direction, turning his eyes away from the Doctor all the while.

Dr. Ngambu smiled thinly as she finished.

"You're a tough old fool, Jakob. What wonders we could have made out of Africa if your people and mine could have worked together!"

Laurence was on his feet again and rapidly regaining strength. He insisted on helping with the construction of shelters in spite of Michelle's protests.

Alison worked alongside Eric as he laid up the poles and covered them with interwoven branches.

There had been no more rumblings of the volcano, but a plume of steam and smoke continued rising slowly from the crater. The smell of sulfur remained heavy in the air.

As soon as Mary Hastings had a break in her duties, Eric and Alison approached her. She looked up at them, wrinkling her nose with a characteristic smile.

"This place smells like a London fog down by the iron works. Africa has something for everybody!"

"Mary," said Eric, "Alison reminded me that you said you knew some of the Turnabo chiefs. How could we locate some of them and arrange for guides to Nairobi? What do you think?"

Mary looked doubtful.

"I had considered the same thing myself, but gave up the idea. It's been such a long time. The old chiefs are probably dead, although I did get to know some of the younger people also. I had only one really strong friendship. That was with an old chief named Mrambah. But his territory was at least a hundred miles from here. Anyone who could claim acquaintance with Mrambah, however, might stand a chance even if he is dead. He was a powerful chief. I knew his son, too, who might even be in his father's place by now."

"If there's any chance at all—"

"I'll think about it. At best, it would still be very dangerous. The Turnabo people are utterly unpredictable. I'll think about it," she said again.

As Mary moved away to look at another patient, Alison shook her head.

"We mustn't persuade her to do it. You can see she believes it would be a death sentence for anyone to go out there—and she would be the first to go."

"In spite of that, some of us may have to take the chance. We can't stay here forever while planes may be searching five hundred miles from here. No matter how you look at it, we can't just sit here. I think God expects us to use the information we have and take action on our own."

"Not entirely," said Alison quietly. "Not without praying."

Eric gave her a quick hug. He was glad for her reminder. This was one of those times he needed her to pray for him. Typically, he had confidence in prayers he could help God answer. But the odds from a strictly human viewpoint were getting bigger and bigger. There was so little anyone could do. "How does one count on God at a time like this?" Eric asked himself aloud.

By afternoon the pall of smoke from the volcano had darkened the sky. The sun shone as if through a murky, yellow film. The dense sulfur fumes made eyes water and nostrils burn. Most of the passengers had begun coughing, some violently. Dampened cloths were tied like surgeon's masks to cover the nose and mouth and cool the burning eyes.

The earth rumblings began again in midafternoon. These were small at first, like the teasings of a giant, then gradually they increased and grew stronger. They came every half hour or less, and it became difficult to stand upright against them.

Animals in the surrounding plain and forest were responding in terror to the quaking earth and smoke. They could be seen from time to time running frantically through the tall grass. Their cries and wailings were frightening to hear, like the howling of dogs that sense some doom approaching.

Captain McGuire and his crew urged everyone to get under the protection of the acacia bough shelters. He instructed them further to exert themselves as little as possible in order to cut down the inhalation of the poisonous fumes.

The injured were already protected as much as possible. Dr. Ngambu, Mary Hastings, and the stewards were in constant attendance. The Doctor seemed scarcely aware of the fury of the rumblings building up in the earth as he went about his duties. Sarah Lander stood by, her eyes constantly on his tall, dignified figure— and watering uncontrollably from the smoke.

Eric helped David and Lars dress the antelope carcasses which had been brought back from the morning hunt. The two naturalists worked swiftly while they tried to suppress their own discomfort.

"Do you think the volcano will blow?" asked Eric.

126

"There's no way of telling," said David. "Sometimes these things will smoke for weeks without erupting. Then again, it might blow its top and cover everything with soda ash six feet deep for forty miles around."

"We've had it if that happens."

"We've had it," David agreed grimly. "Fortunately, they don't often do that. The fall of soda is usually fairly light. It drifts in the atmosphere for many miles. But it's suffocating. We'd lose more patients."

"We can't stay here, can we? There's just no way. Mary thinks it's pretty hopeless to try to get Turnabo guides to take us through their country, but we've got to chance it anyway, haven't we?"

David smiled. "I expected you would reach that conclusion, Eric. That's what we're going to do. As soon as this volcano settles down, I'm going to try for it. I'm taking that big Australian, Mike Ainsworth, and those two Americans, Joe Desmond and Harry Maxwell. I've been watching them. They're tough enough and levelheaded enough to go. Mike and Harry are good shots."

"But I want to go!" Eric protested.

"I kind of thought that's what you had in mind," David said kindly. "Look—we've got to have people back here who can hold up this end, too. You're one of them. Captain McGuire needs you. So does Alison and Dr. Ngambu and Lars. He's staying, too, you know.

"And then, if we don't make it, somebody else is going to have to make a last-ditch try. Lars will lead out with a second party if nothing is heard from us within fifty days. You'll be with that group. OK?"

"You sound like our chances are pretty slim."

"They are, Eric. Very slim. Nobody knows where we are. If they're searching, they're so far off they'll never find us. We've got five hundred miles of hostile native country between us and the nearest civilization. I wouldn't want to bet very much on our chances. There's no use telling the others that, but we've got to face it."

As David looked at him grimly, Eric realized this was what he himself had known for the past several days, but didn't want to admit.

He tried to smile.

"Thanks," he said. "Thanks for leveling with me like that. Not everyone would trust me after the crazy things I've done. I'll be holding up my end, wherever you say."

David sighed, "I know you will, Eric."

They finished dressing the carcasses and began cutting steaks and roasts for the next meals.

It began again during the night. The rumbling had subsided for a while near sunset. Then, as darkness thickened and everybody except those who were standing guard bedded down for the night, the low rumbling began again.

It reminded Alison of the distant thunder of the freight trains she used to hear passing through their hometown of Ivy when she was a little girl. When she sometimes went down to the station at noon, she could feel the earth tremble as the hundred-car freights moved through on their endless journeys.

It was like that now. The sound, and then the feeling in the earth. And then it was beyond all that—like the thunder of jets leaving the earth, and lightning storms in the sky.

"Eric—!"

He crawled over beside her. "Take it easy, Sis. Just take it easy."

"If it blows it could bury us all!"

"It could—but maybe it won't. Let's talk to God about it again."

They remained silent for minutes, comforting each other and pouring out their hearts in a plea to God for safety and preservation.

Then the world exploded.

9 • *Eric Makes a Promise*

Through the leaves of the woven shelter, Eric saw a tower of flame reach for the sky from the distant mountain. Alison clung to him and together they watched the awful spectacle.

A dim, orange light flickered over the landscape. A vast wind rippled the grass and rocked the flimsy shelters. The animals squealed in their fear and roared their defiance as they raced through the waving grass.

A mile-wide fountain of steam and ash poured upward out of the fiery peak. From a crimson base it grew ghostly as it spread in a giant umbrella in the upper layers of the atmosphere. The red glow of the crater tinted it pink on the underside.

Laurence and Michelle crept over to be near the twins and huddled close by, all four clinging to one another.

The first shower of particles sounded like hail on the leaves of the lean-to shelter. It peppered with stinging force and dropped through onto the frightened watchers. Sulphur fumes flowed over them in poisonous waves.

The glow on the mountain diminished and the rumblings faded. Then the ash began to fall in abundance. It shredded the leaves of the flimsy protecting wall. It curled underneath the shelter like smoke and stole the air from their nostrils.

"I can't breathe!" Michelle cried. "My lungs—"

"Don't talk!" Eric commanded. "Keep your face in the mask!"

Beside him, Alison was gasping for breath and trying to hold back her sobs. His own lungs felt as if they were bursting as he held his breath as long as possible. He remembered the time in the pool at Central High when he had gotten a cramp out in the middle of the water and couldn't get his head up. Only the help of a couple of other guys had gotten him safely out.

Now there was no one to get any of them out. There was nothing they could do for one another. They lay huddled with their faces hidden in the almost futile masks, struggling for air in the ocean of soda dust.

How long he had lain there Eric did not know. It seemed hours, but he knew it must have been minutes. As the dust swirled over them, there seemed to be occasional pockets of cleaner air. He filled his lungs in such a moment and looked at his companions. Dimly, he could see them sharing the struggle for breath.

He turned over, holding the nearly dry cloth to his face. The firelight was feeble, almost suffocated by the dust. Its faint light filtered through the haze that drifted like fog. And in that dimness Eric glimpsed a tall, slowly moving figure. Ngambu!

The Doctor was still on his feet checking his patients, wetting their makeshift masks. His own surgeon's mask was clotted with dust.

Eric couldn't believe the persistence and dedication of the man. He touched Alison and whispered in a choked voice.

"I'm going to help the Doctor. Lie still." He got up and staggered from the sheltered area.

He paused a moment to get his bearings and to let the sudden wave of dizziness pass. As he stood, a gunshot rang out. He thought at first it was another blast of the volcano. But it didn't sound like that. And while he looked about for the source of the sound, Dr. Ngambu slowly turned half around and fell to the earth.

But before the Doctor had fallen, an answering gunshot came from somewhere among the shelters. There was a cry of pain from the direction of the first shot. Two more bursts came from that point.

Then two shots erupted simultaneously from the shelter. There was a second cry of pain. And nothing more.

Fighting for breath, passengers struggled to see what new terror was upon them. Most slumped back, face to their near-useless masks once more. Whatever was happening would have to happen.

Eric staggered forward, trying to run. He reached the Doctor's side just as Sarah Lander knelt by him. She was crying behind the mask she held to her face. "I'll kill them all!" she raged in her grief. "I'll kill them all if he's dead. He's the one person in all this useless batch of humanity that deserves to live!"

Eric bent down and listened to the Doctor's heartbeat. "He's alive," he said with gasping breath. "He's breathing. He's hit in the shoulder. Help me get him over to his pad. Take his feet. I'll lift his shoulders."

The Doctor was heavy. They were forced to half carry, half drag his long body toward the shelter. There, he moaned and opened his eyes briefly. Eric tore off the Doctor's surgeon's mask, washed it quickly in a covered container of water, and placed it back over his face. Then, with the light of a flashlight which the Doctor kept nearby, he looked at the wound. It was in the shoulder but very low. He dreaded that it might have pierced a lung.

"See if Mary can come," he said to Sarah.

Sarah nodded and crawled a little distance. But Mary Hastings was already aroused by the shots and had seen the Doctor fall. Both of them scarcely able to stand, she and Sarah crawled toward the Doctor and Eric.

Eric helped Mary dampen her mask and retie it around her face. Gasping for breath, Mary used both hands to cut back the Doctor's shirt and wash the wound. She doused it with antiseptic and taped a dressing to it.

"That will have to do until morning," she said weakly. "I think he's all right. It looks like the bullet missed the bone, and I don't think it hit the lung. But we'll have to get that slug out."

As she spoke, the Doctor's eyes opened narrowly. He seemed to recognize those present. Feebly, his hand dragged away the mask, and his lips formed a smile.

"They didn't get me yet, did they?"

His eyes closed, and the smile faded. Eric replaced the mask and looked questioningly at Mary.

"He'll be all right," said Mary. "If only this air would clear—God, we need Your help. We need to know You're right here with us," she prayed between gasps for air.

Daylight scarcely made any difference. The sky remained almost black, although the air near the ground was becoming a little more breathable as the dust settled out of it and morning winds dispersed it.

It was like a faint twilight when the sun finally began to appear from behind the south shoulder of the volcanic mountain. Eric stirred and looked at the Doctor. He had not moved during the night. Mary was sitting up now and looking at the Doctor with concern.

"He's lost blood. He ought to have an IV. And we haven't got one. We haven't got anything! You get hurt here—you die here!"

She was close to hysteria.

"We have to do what we can," said Eric quietly. "Could we make a little broth for him by boiling some meat in some water—maybe chopping it up fine so he could eat a little of the meat?"

"That would be fine, Eric." Mary was in control of herself once more. "We all feel the same—like we're about to flip—Here we are, Lord," she continued, "needing a lot more cope for today."

Sarah stopped near them.

"I want to see the scum that we shot last night," she said. "I've got a pretty good idea who they were. They've been watching me with fire in their eyes since we got here."

She walked slowly to where the two bodies lay and glanced closely at them. She returned to Dr. Ngambu's

134

side. "They're some of the ones I suspected. One of them is still alive," she announced.

"We'll take care of the Doctor first," said Mary.

"Who fired the second shot, Sarah? You didn't fire twice that second time, did you?" Eric asked.

"I suppose it was Patterson. He was on guard."

"I just learned from the Captain that Patterson was unconscious. He passed out in the cloud of dust."

"Then who—?"

They turned to glance beyond the row of pads in the lean-to. In the next shelter Jakob Vroorman was watching them, his hand clutching a rifle.

"You fired that other shot!" exclaimed Sarah.

"Yaah. Who else did you think?" demanded the Afrikaner sourly.

"We're very grateful to you. You helped save Dr. Ngambu's life."

"Yaah," grunted Vroorman again. "I don't want anybody else getting that nigger Doctor. If anybody gets him it's going to be me!"

Alison and Michelle worked quietly to prepare the meat broth. Dr. Ngambu was conscious enough for Mary to spoon-feed it to him. He seemed to relish it, and it strengthened him considerably.

"We have some good cooks around here," he said. Then he added, "What about the fellow that shot me?"

"There were two of them," said Eric. "One's dead."

"The other one?"

"Still alive. Probably wounded too badly to live."

"Ah," said Dr. Ngambu. "We must do something for the poor fellow. Please bring him over, and I will see if I can tell you what you must do."

Eric started to protest. The Doctor held up a hand weakly.

"I know. He shot me. Bring him over to me just the same."

Eric and David brought the man over to Dr. Ngambu. He was dark, apparently an Arabian of unknown nationality. He spoke English. The Doctor saw at once the chest wound, near the heart, was fatal under the circumstances. Perhaps in a well equipped hospital—

There was nothing to be done.

"You tried to kill me," the Doctor said gently. "I have done nothing to you. I would heal your wound if I could."

"Nothing!" The words seemed to explode from the man. "You call this nothing?" He waved a hand feebly toward the survivors clustered in the camp. "Except for you all of us would be safe in our cities of comfort. Here we lie dying in this desert—because of you! You must die. You *will* die! Others will see to that!"

His wild, fanatic voice stilled as blood gushed suddenly from his mouth, and his head lolled forward.

Sarah murmured, "One man's reason is another's insanity. That's what we're faced with. He meant it—they won't give up even after we're rescued."

Dr. Ngambu nodded. "I knew that the moment our plane was hit. They will pursue me until either I or they are dead."

"Surely your own secret police can handle this when you are back home?" said Eric.

"Perhaps. A few more names added to my list of enemies will make little difference in the end. I wonder how many more of *them* are here among us now. We eat with *them* and talk with *them* and do business with *them*. But they turn and stab us when they don't like our actions or our thoughts—or what we are. And so we are forced to kill or be killed. Is there no end to it?"

"It began when the world began," said Mary. "The insane, the prejudiced, the cocky ones who want to own the world—they've always been with us. Maybe in the end they *will* own the world."

Dr. Ngambu smiled and shook his head slightly.

"No, Mary, they won't. In the end good men will win. It just takes a little longer to do it with honor."

His head slumped. Alarmed, Eric bent down. Mary brushed him away.

"The Doctor is all right. But he's exhausted. He's had far too much strain already. We must leave him alone."

"The mask?" said Sarah.

Mary dipped the mask again and laid it over the Doctor's face.

"He'll be fine," she said.

But Eric insisted on staying beside him. He was glad he did, because Dr. Ngambu awakened in about an hour and reached for his hand.

"Eric, I want you to do something for me. These documents I am carrying in this leather envelope contain the final takeover procedures for my government in Niroona."

Eric helped him unfasten the holster that contained the portfolio.

"I do not want them destroyed because they provide the only written document for history to prove our intentions for a bloodless takeover. Please wear them under your shirt as I have done. I know that you and your sister are the grandchildren of E. Bradford Thorne. He should be very proud of you both. See that these papers get into the right hands with his help.''

The shoulder holster was still warm from the Doctor's body as Eric slipped it on.

"One thing more," Dr. Ngambu said. "If you cannot fulfill your promise, do not worry. I am sure God will vindicate us—in His time.''

Captain McGuire and David had both been so overcome by the sulfur fumes and soda ash that they were nearly unconscious during the time of the shooting and for a long time after. They had been only very dimly aware of anything going on. This was also the case with half the camp. Four of the injured and three others had died during the night.

The fumes and dust still swirled about the camp, pouring over the edge of the precipice in visible torrents and then being hurled upward by currents of air to sweep over the camp again as if in strangling vengeance. The dampened cloth masks were still worn as a feeble protection against the menace.

Without Dr. Ngambu to attend the patients, Mary Hastings and her crew worked desperately. Alison, Michelle, Sarah, and several others assisted. The exposure to the fumes and dust had weakened all those struggling to survive their injuries. Mary was afraid they were going to lose another four or five in addition to those who had died during the night.

The white soda ash covered everything like a blanket of snow. It was five or six inches deep on the ground.

Walking in it caused a cloud to rise up and stifle whoever was in it. Captain McGuire organized a task force to devise some broad scrapers out of brush, which they used to push much of the soda over the edge of the cliff and clear the camp space.

By noontime the sky was still covered by a charcoal gray curtain. The light of the campfire was still required. Throughout the day the animal sounds never ceased. The beasts continued their fearful screaming and howling, as if stirred to some primitive battle charge.

Then, toward evening, one sound began to swell above the others, a shrill screeching and howling that sent a chill through Alison and Michelle, and made Sarah shudder.

"What animal is that?" Sarah asked.

"You've got me," said Eric. "David must know." He called out to the naturalist.

"Baboons. They get awfully excited over any natural disturbance."

"There must be a million of them," said Alison.

"I hope not." David paused and listened somberly. "They're nasty creatures when they get riled. I've never heard so many before. It does sound like hundreds, at least."

"What can they do?" said Alison.

"Normally, nothing—except to each other, and to animals they prey on. But once in a while, when they get real excited, they will attack a man. When they do—well, a lion attack is no worse. Baboons are among the fiercest, meanest animals alive. In a rage they go completely berserk."

Alison shuddered.

"I hope they don't come this way."

David's eyes tried to pierce the dimness from where the chilling sounds came.

"Yes—I'm hoping with you that they don't." He left to join Lars and Captain McGuire. Eric guessed they were talking about the baboon horde.

Michelle seemed overwhelmed by despair. "Maybe those were right who went back to the plane. Maybe we'd all have been better off down there."

"We'd have been dead by now," said Eric. "As I'm sure those men are who went down last night. We've come this far. We have to go on from here."

The cries of the baboons rose in a burst of terrifying screams. They were echoed by cries of despair from among the passengers. Eric wondered if it would be another night of threat—from either the baboons or the volcano. Or both. He looked up at the ominous mountain. Its peak glowed once again with a crescent of reddish light. The rumblings of the earth had come and gone throughout the day. They could be felt faintly now. Night was coming on with a gathering of terrors.

By nightfall Dr. Ngambu was much improved. He was able to give directions to Mary and those helping her in caring for their patients, including himself. Everyone was exhausted and ill from the fumes and dust, but they kept up with camp duties as best they could. Captain McGuire and David were among those hardest hit, but they were fairly well recovered by the end of the day.

Sunset made little difference. It was scarcely darker

140

than before. A scanty meal was prepared of antelope meat and broth. The meat had to be washed of dust. Fresh water had to be brought. The spring had been contaminated by soda ash, but had cleaned itself by now.

A night guard was set up, and the camp bedded down amid the fearful jungle sounds and the almost constant rumbling of the earth beneath them. Eric urged Alison and Michelle to get some sleep, but they continued working with Mary for another two hours.

The baboon horde quieted somewhat, and Eric fell into a sleep that left him feeling guilty when he finally awoke toward morning. He had not heard Alison and Michelle go to bed, nor had he been aware of anything else in the camp.

Then he realized that what had wakened him was a dull boom of thunder from the mountain. He jerked himself up in time to see a plume of flame burst again from its peak. It was a small eruption, however, a mere burp compared with the previous one, he thought.

But it sent the animals into a frenzy. The howlings and screeches reached new highs as if the animals had reached limits of their endurance. Their frantic rushing about in the trees and the tall grass seemed to be coming closer.

Eric got up and joined in building up the fire. He saw David and Lars and some of the plane crew patrolling about, guns in hand, peering into the dimness of the grassland beyond.

Suddenly David shouted. "They're coming! Everybody around the fire. The baboons are charging!"

10 • *Volcanoes, Baboons, and Drums*

With frightened cries, the camp members ran for the protection of the fire—all except the injured, unable to move. Alison and Michelle ran to join Mary and Sarah and the stewards at the side of those.

"Eric!" David called. "Light torches! Pass them around and make a line outside the shelters!"

Eric understood. He plunged short branches into the fire and lifted out some that were already burning. He handed one to the nearest person, a short, pudgy man who shrank back when offered the torch.

"Take this!" Eric demanded in sudden anger. "Get out there with David and the Captain to hold off those animals!"

Sweat stood out on the man's forehead.

"Those beasts will kill us all." His hands trembled.

"They sure will if we don't drive them off. Take it—get out there!"

The man grasped it and ran, terrified, toward the

line beyond the shelters. Eric handed three more to other hesitant and reluctant men. Then a tall, young woman stepped up.

"Give me one!" she demanded.

Eric smiled at her strong, angry face.

"Thanks," he said. "Maybe you can find some more like you to help out."

She did. The woman dragged up four more of her companions who grasped torches and ran to the line forming against the massed baboon horde in the grass.

The cries of the crazed animals seemed all about them now. New thunders burst from the mountain. The fire burned higher as Eric and his companions added fuel. Between it and the edge of the precipice most of the company of survivors huddled.

A rifle shot rang out from somewhere on the defense line. The animal cries seemed to change to shrieks of rage. The baboons charged the defenders in a blind rush.

Eric grabbed one of the burning torches and ran to the defense line. David and others with guns were firing rapidly now, dropping the animals as they leaped over dead bodies of their fellows to get to the men. Eric swung the fiery torch in the faces of the beasts. They seemed scarcely to notice the fire, swatting the flames with their paws.

Eric backed and stumbled as a giant animal lunged toward him. Its powerful swing knocked the torch from his hand, and it leaped into the air, its thick, hairy arms outstretched.

A crack of rifle fire sounded a dozen feet away. The animal crashed to the ground, its black, primitive face twisted in pain. Eric couldn't help thinking what a beautiful creature it was—and feeling sorrow for its wasteful death.

David's voice shouted from what seemed a vast distance. "Get back, Eric! They're going to rush again!"

Eric scrambled to his feet and ran to the fire for another torch. All those he had placed earlier were burning now. He forced them into the hands of reluctant passengers standing nearby.

"Hold those animals back!"

He raced back to the line. The hunters were firing less rapidly now. To Eric, the baboons seemed to be falling back, confused by the sprawled bodies of their dead comrades. In the distant grass others continued to howl. While his eyes watched the nightmare, another part of Eric's mind wondered how many days' supply of ammunition had been used up.

A cry of terror came suddenly from the other end of the camp where the patients lay under the shelters.

Mary Hastings cried out, "Help us! Oh, help us over here!"

The animals had attacked near that end while the defenders had been drawn from that part of the camp.

David and Eric raced to the area, just in time to see a cluster of black, furry bodies dancing away, and in the center of their group—something else. Something that looked and sounded like a man screaming in pain and terror.

"It was Mr. Darnelles, the American contractor," cried Mary. "They just swooped in here, chittering and howling, and dragged him away."

144

David's rifle cracked a half dozen times in the direction of the fleeing black bodies. They faded into the night. The main horde drained away and followed after.

"There's no way—there's just no way to get him back—" David's voice shook in bitter despair.

Eric remembered the man, Howard Darnelles. His leg had been nearly severed in the crash, but Dr. Ngambu thought there might be a chance of saving it even yet if they could get him to a hospital.

His cry of terror echoed in Eric's mind. Alison and Michelle were standing near Mary, their arms about each other.

Abruptly, Dr. Ngambu was beside them, looking out into the blackness. No one had seen him rise from where he was lying.

"It is mine," he said. "I carry the weight of all this on my shoulders. I would gladly give myself to the animals if I could wipe it all out."

The baboons retreated until their cries could scarcely be heard. Dawn came at last, a little brighter now. Hardly anyone in the camp had moved from the frozen positions they had taken during the attack. Dr. Ngambu shuffled along painfully to the fire and arranged some breakfast meat on the spits over the flames. Many of the passengers avoided looking at him. An angry murmur or two was heard. Dr. Ngambu faced the direction of the sound and bowed his head.

Finally the defense line was dismantled. David retreated alone to the edge overlooking the Valley. Captain McGuire approached him.

"I want to say thanks, David. You saved the camp last night."

David rubbed his face savagely with his fingers.

"Darnelles—I keep hearing him calling out. I should have protected that end. I was watching their main attack and left it open. They could have grabbed off a dozen people."

"Don't blame yourself. You *saved* many dozens of people. We have to keep going. We're still a long way from home."

"We must be ready to start for Nairobi as soon as the volcano cools and the animal threat dies out. Even then, I hate to take any firepower and manpower from the camp."

"I'm talking about *now*," said the Captain. "I think you should leave at once. Never mind what the volcano or the animals are going to do. We could wait for months for those threats to go away. And each day's delay means another day these people are cut-off from the help they need. I'd like you to finish preparations today and be on your way tomorrow morning. Do you disagree?"

David remained silent a long time and then finally shook his head slowly.

"No. I can't disagree. We're really up a creek any way you look at it. But you've got to remember, too, that our chances of getting through Turnabo territory aren't exactly the best in the world."

"I know. That's just one more of the chances we have to take."

"I've lined up Lars and Eric to take a second party out if we don't get word back to you on schedule."

146

"Good. But I know you can get through if anybody can."

"We'll pull out in the morning."

"Thanks, David."

Eric learned of the advance in plans from David. "There's no guarantee things are going to get better here—and maybe they're going to get worse. I only wish I could go with you."

"You may get your chance."

"Not *that* way—not based upon your failure. You're going to get through!"

Word spread quickly throughout the camp that David's expedition was going to leave at once. The news seemed to lighten the spirits of the passengers considerably, even those who had been most critical and noncooperative. It didn't matter that they might have to wait nearly two months for any results. Knowing that something was being done was encouraging.

Eric found Dr. Ngambu had returned to his pad to lie down because of pain and fever. Eric sat beside him. Soda dust swirled in the beams of sunlight filtering from the sky.

"Is there anything I can do for you?" asked Eric.

The Doctor shook his head. His glasses were no longer poised on the bridge of his nose. Eric remembered they had disappeared the night he was shot.

"There's nothing you can do, Eric. The ladies are performing their jobs as nurses very well. Maybe I could enlist you as a surgeon, however," he said with faint humor. "This bullet needs to come out, and Mary says she can't do it. It's deep. We have no anesthetic left. Even if I had what they stole to use on young Laurence there would not be enough."

"Can't it wait until we get out of here?"

"It seems to be exerting pressure on a nerve, and there's infection developing around it. I can't bear it much longer, I'm afraid."

"If Mary would try it—is there anything I or anyone else could do to help her?"

Dr. Ngambu smiled.

"You've got guts enough to try, haven't you?"

"It's not that. I'd do anything I could to help you."

"I'll see. If I can get back some more strength in another day or two, we may have to seriously consider it—and I may take you up on your offer. I think you just might make a passable surgeon."

"You've done more than enough for the rest of us. It's time we did something for you."

Dr. Ngambu laughed bitterly.

"Yes, I've done so much, haven't I? I've nearly killed you all. That poor fellow, Darnelles—I'll hear his voice for the rest of my life."

It was no use arguing with the Doctor, Eric knew. He would blame himself the rest of his life for the disaster to the plane and its people. He was that kind of man.

But Eric tried again. "I think we should set our goal to make everything as right as we possibly can now. 'Looking back and blaming or excusing what's past can cloud the present and destroy the future.' That's what Gramps says."

Dr. Ngambu patted his arm gently.

"Keep doing that, Eric, and you'll be all right.

148

For me, it's just that my account is so very much in the red right now. I've got a lot of making up to do—so very much making up to do—"

His eyes closed in weariness as his head turned to one side. Eric sat looking at him for a long time. What a world it would be, he thought, if it were made up of Ngambus. The strong-boned face was like an ebony rock. The eyes, now closed, seemed to see beyond the range of vision of anyone else around him.

Eric hoped that when this was all over he would have a chance to know Dr. Ngambu better.

He left the Doctor and approached Mary Hastings, who had been feeding a patient nearby.

"Dr. Ngambu says that bullet is going to have to come out," he said.

"Are you a surgeon?" snapped Mary. Then she apologized immediately. "I didn't mean to snap at you that way. I know he needs it out. I know it more than he does. I've done a lot of nursing in my time, but I'm not a surgeon. I just couldn't go probing in such a difficult position while that man is lying there with no anesthetic. It's stupid, I know. I should be able to do it—"

"Mary—maybe this sounds even more stupid, but is there anything that maybe you and I could do together? He *needs* help—"

The woman looked at him quietly. Her eyes moistened.

"You really want to help him, don't you?"

Eric nodded.

"Let's talk about it tomorrow. And be thinking about how it would be, tying him down and then probing deep and painfully while he's trying to keep from screaming with pain."

There had been a small movement of air during the morning, but in the afternoon it ceased completely. Only the fine settling of soda ash particles continued. The heat seemed trapped under the layer of dust that obscured the sun. It was as oppressive now as it had been in the Valley.

The distant animals seemed restless again. Their cries began rising on the still, heated air, as if carrying the threat of something fearful and disastrous.

Alison said, "It's like the way the horses were on Grandpa's farm back home before a summer lightning storm."

The members of the camp felt an uneasiness that kept them looking around, over their shoulders, for something that might be ready to spring upon them. The smell of sulfur was suffocating.

David ordered the fire built up again. The supply of fuel was not great. It had not been replenished since the baboon attack. Eric stockpiled a supply of branches for torches if they should be needed again.

Shortly afterward, a series of quakes shook the camp for several minutes. Everyone glanced fearfully at the mountain. The crimson glow at its peak could be seen faintly. Then, as they watched, that glow slowly became brighter and edged over the lip of the crater.

"Lava!" someone screamed.

The mountain thundered. The vibration shook the watchers off their feet and sprawled them on the ground. Some of them began sobbing.

150

Alison crawled close to Eric.

"Is it going to cover the camp with lava?"

"I don't think anyone knows the answer to that. All I know is that the volcanoes in this area produce little lava. It's mostly steam and ash. But here we've got a lava dome."

An explosion like the sustained blast of a rocket engine erupted and sent a new stream of fire rising from the mountain. Eric watched closely and finally breathed a sigh of relief. "That looked more like steam than anything else. We may not get another shower of dust out of this."

"Lava is better?" Alison asked.

"It's not a big flow. Look, it's already slowing down."

Then, as they watched, a new wave burst over the lip of the crater and raced down the side of the mountain in flaming fury, cremating every living plant and creature in its way.

Eric felt sick. It could even reach the campsite. He reminded himself it was farther away than it seemed—a good twenty-five miles between that lava tongue and where they lay. The flow would cool and surge and cool again—it would take days if it came at all. And then where would they be if the camp were wiped out?

Alison and Michelle were trying to comfort each other. Eric and Laurence looked at each other across the frightened girls.

"Is this the end of it?" Laurence asked in resignation.

"No!" Eric exclaimed. "This is not the end of it. No matter what happens tonight the party is leaving tomorrow for Nairobi. And the rest of us hang on right here until rescue comes. Listen," Eric said intensely, "there's more to hanging on than just staying alive. Do you know that?"

"No," said Laurence. "What more is there?"

"Him." Eric jerked an arm in the direction of Dr. Ngambu. "There's a man whose whole purpose lies in making up for what he thinks was his responsibility in the plane crash. He'd laugh if I called him a saint, but that's what he is. We owe it to him to stay alive, if nothing else."

Laurence glanced toward the Doctor.

"So every death is another debt he can never repay?"

"That's it. I have my own reasons for wanting him to survive. So do you. But there's a bigger one to add to all the other reasons: Don't add to the Doctor's burden. So don't ask me or yourself or anyone else if this is all. It isn't until you say it is."

Others around them were slowly getting to their feet as the trembling of the earth diminished. All eyes stared with dreadful fascination at the creeping, bloodred scar on the side of the mountain. Eric knew that lava flows sometimes move as fast as fifty miles per hour, or more, but this one showed no signs yet of such fury.

It was still hours to sunset, but the added flood of ash in the upper layers of the atmosphere was closing off the sunlight again. It was like a total eclipse at midday.

The animal cries did not diminish. Rather, they increased in volume and frenzy. Above all the rest, Eric thought he heard the one dreaded sound of the night before—the vast troop of baboons.

His fears were confirmed.

David shouted, "The baboons are coming back! Bring torches! Guns on the line!"

Panic struck the camp. Passengers rushed again to the space between the fire and the precipice. Eric thrust the branches into the fire and passed out already burning torches. David and the rest of the gun bearers took up their positions beyond the lean-tos. They began firing almost at once as the first wave of baboons raged toward them.

"Get those torches here!" David shouted.

Eric shoved them into the hands of those nearby. Some died out and had to be returned to the flame.

David raced back for a moment.

"Eric—" He stared at the small pile of firewood and torches. "Is this all we've got left?"

"That's all."

David hesitated an instant, then shouted above the chaos of animal and human voices, "Clear the injured back to the campfire. You have four minutes. We've got to fire the lean-tos."

"David—" Eric gasped.

"Here—take my pistol. We haven't got enough fire out there to do any good. Get up to the line with me."

David glanced at his watch as the injured were being dragged on their litters toward the fire. He turned and shot into the mass of frenzied, enraged bodies. Some of them had already spilled over into the campground. He knelt and took swift aim, firing carefully and swiftly, recognizing the danger to people on the other side of the cluster of baboons.

The animals squealed as some of their companions dropped. They raced back to the line outside.

"Torch the lean-tos!" David commanded.

The half dozen people who held torches reluctantly obeyed. They plunged their fire into the half-dried leaves and branches. There was a moment when it looked as if nothing would burn. Then the flames caught, and a wall of fire sprang up behind the gunners. Eric took his place alongside them.

"Make every shot count!" David cried.

They worked the guns as rapidly as possible, but the sea of black bodies seemed endless. The baboons advanced in shrieking, fanatic rage. One of them lunged through the air at Eric as on the night before. Eric fired in time for the beast to drop at his feet, its weight rolling against him, knocking him to the ground.

"Get back," David called. "They're coming in. Don't let them break through—"

Eric scrambled to his feet. The heat of the burning brush wall at his back pierced his shirt and broiled his skin. Yet he had to fall back before the onslaught of the animals. David pulled him into the narrow passage between two of the shelters. The flames licked at them.

"In here," David said.

"We can't let them—"

"In here!"

Eric obeyed, knowing that in a moment the flames would die, and the animals would rush through. He coughed and closed his eyes a moment against the stinging smoke. Then a new sound broke upon his ears.

He listened, then turned to David.

"You hear that?"

The naturalist was already listening.

"Drums. Human voices—"

11 • The Message of the Two Spears

Eric peered through the opening the baboons had made in the undergrowth. The remaining firelight illuminated not only the furry animal bodies, but, beyond them, the glistening ebony bodies of men.

Men carrying long spears and wearing tribal headdress and padding fiercely on drums suspended about their necks.

"Turnabo!" exclaimed David. "It must be the Turnabo!"

"They seem to be driving off the baboons."

The natives were prodding the animals with their spears, but were not harming them.

"They're herding them," said Eric. "The baboons don't attack them."

David wiped his face with a grimy hand and lowered his rifle. "Savage or not, those tribesmen have just saved us from the baboons."

David started to laugh. Eric laughed with him, and

they pounded each other on the back and felt a little craziness in themselves for a minute.

"Let's get Mary," said David at last. "Maybe she can understand what's going on with the natives. We ought to find some way to say thanks to them for saving our lives."

They found Mary with the patients who had been hastily and painfully moved. She stood stone-still listening to the drums and the whooping and chanting of the natives who had dispersed the baboons.

"They saved our lives," said David. "We ought to somehow say thanks to them."

Mary remained stony faced. Then at last she turned and spoke. "The Turnabo do no favors. They are not a friendly people."

"Then why did they chase off the baboons just as they were about to overrun us?"

"I don't know." She listened again. "I'm trying to understand their chant. As near as I can tell, it's a kind of death chant, an offering to the Sleeping Devil who lives in the mountain."

"Now I remember. I've heard this chant before. This mountain—they call it the Mountain of the Sleeping Devil."

"The volcano?"

"Yes."

"Has that got anything to do with us?"

"I think so. And I don't think we're going to like the answer, whatever it is."

Eric felt a stab of fear in his stomach. The native chant sounded as if hundreds were out there. Turnabo deliberately went about clearing a space and lighting a fire of their own. Their dancing and chanting and brandishing of spears to the beat of deep, vibrant drums echoed the thunder of the mountain itself. It was a monotonous, pounding, numbing sound that somehow held the threat of death in its beat. Their voices increased in tempo to the point of mad, jangling hysteria.

Alison came over.

"They frighten me. What are they doing?"

"I wish I knew," said Mary fervently. "I wish I knew."

The tribesmen indicated no intention of making further contact. Their hysterical chanting and dancing continued far into the evening. The maddening sound pounded through the air and beat against the eardrums until one or two of the passengers began screaming in their own hysteria for it to stop.

Captain McGuire and his crew moved among the people trying to reassure them. Dr. Ngambu walked about with painful slowness, refusing Eric's advice to take it easy.

"Do you have any idea what the tribesmen are up to?" Eric asked the Doctor. "Mary says she doesn't understand it."

He nodded, grim faced.

"I think I do."

"Then what is it all about? Or what do you think it means, anyway?"

"Let us wait until we can be sure. When the time comes, we will all know."

Dr. Ngambu moved away, refusing to say more. Eric looked after him, wondering at the Doctor's ominous words. Everything added up to one thing now. The natives were definitely not friendly.

Eric told David what the Doctor had said.

"I think we ought to prepare for an attack from them."

"We don't know for certain that they're going to attack."

"Do you have any doubt about it?"

The naturalist looked at Eric with a grim smile. "Not really. When they've completed their ceremony and worked themselves up to a high enough pitch they'll attack."

"What will we do?"

"Take as many of them with us as we possibly can."

"Are you saying there's no way we can drive them off?"

David looked at Eric steadily with sadness in his eyes. "Eric, there are hundreds of them out there. Maybe as many as a thousand. What chance do you think we've got when they start rushing us? We've got four rifles and six pistols and a couple of shotguns. We can't fire and reload fast enough. We haven't got a chance in the world, Eric. I'm sorry."

"There must be something we can do! It can't— everything can't just end this way!"

"You can tell Alison and the others—or not tell them until it happens—whatever seems best to you. The only other alternative would be to pass the guns out among our own people—for their own use—before the natives strike. It would be more merciful than a spear thrust— or whatever they will do to the ones they take alive."

He turned away, and Eric remained standing,

numbed in mind and body. It didn't seem possible that this was happening. After all they had been through they had a right to a chance for survival. David had to be wrong.

He plodded toward the spot where Alison was seated with Michelle and Laurence. The blood pounded in his head. In rhythm, he thought, with the deafening, hysterical chant of the natives.

"What's wrong with you?" Alison demanded. "You look like you're sick!"

"I guess I am. Alison—Michelle—Laurence—I have just talked with David and Mary and Dr. Ngambu. They believe the Turnabo are hostile. David thinks they are about ready to attack—and that we have no chance whatever against them."

His companions stared as if they had not heard him. "It can't be," Alison murmured at last. "It just can't be."

Michelle stared into the distance. "In a way, I won't mind too much. We'll be with our little Marie, again, won't we?" She turned to Laurence.

He nodded.

"Yes. But I had hoped—" His voice trailed off to silence. "I had hoped and believed we would be rescued even yet."

"Isn't there a single thing we can do?" asked Alison. "We can't just sit here—and wait for them—"

"If the attack comes as David expects, there's no way out for us. We can kill a few score of them, but in the end they'll simply smother us with sheer numbers."

Alison was looking across the camp.

"I see David and Lars and Captain McGuire and his

people talking with Mary and Dr. Ngambu. Maybe they'll come up with something. Oh, Eric—I can't believe it's ending like this!"

He put an arm around her and held her tight.

"Yeah, it does seem crazy, being wiped out here by a savage African tribe."

Alison shivered at the new tone in Eric's voice—listless and passive.

"Back home in Ivy, Mr. Douglas is checking groceries at the supermarket. Brother Michels is getting his Sunday sermon ready. The City Council is still wondering if they should put a traffic light on the interstate by Central High."

"And Dad will be in Nairobi," said Alison, trying to put some spirit in the sad monologue. "I'll bet he's really shaking things up to get us rescued. And Gramps. If only they could have looked in the right place to begin with—"

As they watched, the camp leaders moved toward the fire and called everybody to come up.

"They're going to tell them," said Eric.

From where they sat, Eric and Alison and their friends could hear Captain McGuire's solemn words as he told the group the plight they were in. The tension of the past nine days reached the breaking point with his words of doom. A score of passengers, both men and women, broke into violent sobbing. Some quietly. Some hysterically.

"There isn't much chance that we're wrong," said Captain McGuire. "The intent of the Turnabo seems very clear to those of us who have had much experience in Africa. Such weapons as we have will be used by our

160

best marksmen. We'll hold them back as long as we can. There's nothing more we can do."

He moved away, but the group remained standing in place, as if frozen by his words. The fear and despair was almost a visible thing, hanging like some ghostly shroud over them all, Eric thought.

Alone, unmoving, Dr. Ngambu stood at the far edge of the camp, as if completely removed from all that was going on before him. Eric wondered what thoughts were going through the Doctor's mind at this moment. Then, as he stood there, the members of the camp slowly erupted into a hysterical turbulence.

At the opposite corner of the camp another figure stood in almost the same position as the Doctor. Jakob Vroorman. He stood straight, hands clasped behind his back, his grizzled head erect. He regarded the scene as if he were some stern, remote father viewing the antics of a school of unthinking children. He, too, seemed unconcerned with what was going on.

In a sense, Eric thought, the old Afrikaner was as magnificent as the Doctor. He and his ancestors had fought the whole world for a place of their own in which to live. And the world had fought back at them. Perhaps it was not entirely to his shame that Jakob Vroorman had become a bitter old man.

But if these two could face what lay ahead so calmly and without concern could he do any less, Eric asked himself.

There was little fuel left for the fire, and not many felt like eating, but a few chunks of meat were put on the spits as the sky became completely dark.

"Do you want anything?" Eric asked Alison.

161

She shook her head. "I couldn't eat."

Laurence and Michelle agreed.

"We don't want anything," Laurence said.

The beating of the drums and the howls of the natives continued without letup.

Eric walked over to David and asked if one of the guns would be assigned to him.

"You take one of the pistols," said David. "Here is your share of ammunition."

Eric took the weapon and the pocketful of shells. He wondered if he should save a couple—or four—for the very end.

Abruptly, the shrieking, wailing, maddening sounds from the Turnabo camp ceased. The complete silence that followed was in its own way just as frightening. The natives' fire had been allowed to dim, and it was difficult to see what they were doing. It appeared they were simply kneeling—the many hundreds of them—in concentric circles about the fire. Unmoving, their spears rested upright, clasped firmly in one hand.

While they knelt, a faint swish was heard in the air above the center of the camp. Eyes turned as a slender ebony shaft buried its head in the ground near the fire. A short banner of red fluttered from its tail. A second spear followed the first, planting its banner nearby.

"On line!" David cried. "Hold your fire until I give the signal."

The gunners rushed to their posts at the edge of the ruined shelters. A shower of spears hissed through the air and landed beyond the camp area.

Turnabo warriors remained hidden in the darkness. David waited.

"They'll be up again in a minute," he said. "Don't waste a bullet."

Eric thought of the hundreds the baboon attack had cost them. His pocketful of shells would not hold out long against the Turnabo horde.

It was quiet for long minutes. Then the drums began slowly, building up to a hysteric beat. David crawled to the farthest edge of the camp. Suddenly, the tempo of the drums increased. Terrible war cries pierced the night.

Eric cried aloud. To his left, he saw David writhing on the ground. A needle-sharp shaft of wood protruded from his hip.

"David!"

No sound came in reply.

Eric raised the pistol, firing desperately into the darkness. On either side of him the rifles and pistols and the shotguns blazed. David lay in direct line of fire. He did not move.

On his right, Eric saw Mr. Patterson suddenly fling his hands in the air as he gave a cry of agony and fell back. A spear pierced his chest. Eric continued firing. He flung himself down and began working his way toward the rifle Patterson had dropped.

An unexpected movement and a flash of color to his left startled Eric. He glanced about, missing a shot. There, beyond David, the red banner of one of the two Turnabo spears was held high and moving toward the savages who remained out of sight in the darkness.

The drums kept on in their unceasing rhythm, becoming louder now as the figure with the raised spear moved toward them.

Then a chilling cry of triumph came from Turnabo throats. A line of warriors suddenly appeared, like statues holding their poised spears without throwing them. The drums increased their tempo.

No one moved. It was as though someone had signaled "Freeze!"

A startled voice barked the order, "Hold your fire!"

The figure holding aloft the strange banner appeared slowly. He halted a moment between the lines. Then, in utter silence, Dr. Ngambu moved forward again toward the line of unmoving, ebony warriors.

In panic, Eric shouted to him. "Come back! Doctor! Dr. Ngambu!"

And as he rose to his feet, preparing to run toward this drama, Eric felt strong arms pull him back and knock Patterson's rifle from his hand.

"Get down and shut up!" McGuire growled.

Dr. Ngambu moved on tired and weakened legs. He held out the banner and extended it toward the savages.

The spears came down.

"Hold fire!" cried McGuire in a voice torn with pain and anguish for the doctor.

Ngambu halted before the Turnabo line. He stood a moment, waiting. Then a Turnabo in elaborate head-dress stepped forward, took the spear and banner from him. There was no other movement. The black warriors stood silently, their spears above their heads. The drums continued their beating.

Eric could not control the sobs that came suddenly to his throat. He did not know what was happening, but he knew it was something terrible. He would never be able to forget it as long as he lived.

Abruptly, Dr. Ngambu was seized by the arms and his hands were tied brutally behind his back. He stifled a cry as his wounded shoulder was twisted painfully. For a moment he jerked free and stood straight in powerful majesty that held even his tormentors awed temporarily.

In a loud voice he spoke to his companions in the camp.

"These people believe that the gods of the mountain are displeased. The Sleeping Devil has awakened and spoken his displeasure. He has told them he will be satisfied only with the sacrifice of their enemies. So they have come. They have come to destroy us all. But the Sleeping Devil will be more pleased if two willing sacrifices are brought. That was the message of the two spears with red banners. I have returned one. The other must be brought. Then they will spare the rest of you.

"I have brought all this agony and destruction upon you, my friends. I did not mean to. Now, in this last service that I do, perhaps you can forgive me for the pain and death my presence with you has caused. I pray for your safety."

Ngambu turned. There was a quick exchange of words and gestures between the Doctor and the chief.

Again Ngambu spoke to the camp. "I regret in the depths of my heart that one other must join me or the sacrifice cannot be complete. In no other way can the vengeance of the Sleeping Devil be satisfied."

There was a sickening silence as the shock of this message came through to them.

"No—No! No, you cannot be sacrificed for us!" a man's voice called out.

Mary Hastings could be heard unashamedly praying in desperate tones, her words punctuated by sobs, as she realized the full impact of the savages' demands. Beside her stood Sarah Lander, her hand gripping her automatic as she half raised it toward the Turnabo chieftain.

A sudden movement at the right turned their attention to a figure bursting forth and grasping the second spear. Within seconds the second red banner was held high and moving toward the savage line.

"That nigger doctor is not going to go one better than Jakob Vroorman!" The Afrikaner's voice thundered in a bull-like roar. In the dying firelight, his proud figure limped swiftly toward Dr. Ngambu. Then, with all his might, Vroorman hurled the spear into the ground before the chieftain.

Instantly, angry hands seized and bound his arms painfully tight. He grinned through his agony. "Finally you and I do something together, Doctor!"

12 • One More Question . . .

Like melting shadows, the black figures of the hundreds of tribesmen vanished almost silently into the night. In their midst were their two captives. The Sleeping Devil would be satisfied.

As they left, the chief approached a little way and threw an object toward the camp, intoning something in his own language. Then, with his men, he was gone. Only the dying embers of their fire told that they had once been there.

Numbness filled those in camp. Mechanically, they stirred, moving a few paces from where they stood, then stopping because they did not know where to go. They did not speak to one another. There was the sound of deep sobbing from some.

Coming out of his paralysis, Eric remembered his friend, David.

Captain McGuire was already kneeling by the naturalist when Eric joined him. David was unconscious.

Together, Eric and the Captain turned him over carefully. Eric withdrew the spear easily. It was pointed. It had no barbs.

Mary saw it and choked.

"Poison," she said. "Only when they're poisoned do they use the small, unbarbed shafts."

Lars was there, too. He could not stifle his sobs over his old friend. Eric wanted to hit something. He felt like running insanely into the darkness behind the departing savages and firing his gun into their midst until his cartridges were spent.

He knew what the poisoned shaft meant for David. They had no antidote. The point had gone deep in his flesh just below his hip joint.

They carried him to a spot near the other patients and laid him on a pad of grass. Mary brought a cloth and water and bathed his face.

"He'll be feverish," she said.

"Is there any way to drain the wound?" asked Eric. "Cut it out or suck out the poison?"

"It's all through his body by now. If you got half a drop in your mouth you'd be a goner, too."

Lars knelt by and raised an eyelid of his friend's unseeing eye. Gently he closed it.

"David—David—" he sobbed.

"He may not regain consciousness," said Mary. "It's best that he doesn't. Then he won't feel the pain."

Alison and Sarah joined them. Two and three at a time, they sat beside David throughout the night. Only once did he move. His head turned. A great sound escaped his lips. Then he was still.

Mary bent closer.

"Thank God," she said. "He didn't suffer long."

Eric got up and strode away. A vast emptiness filled him. First Dr. Ngambu, now David. And Jakob Vroorman—there was a greatness there that he had not understood. He buried his face in his hands and hot, stinging tears flowed from his eyes.

After a time he wiped his face with his hands and straightened. He glimpsed then a figure slowly approaching in the dimness. He felt a moment's anger at the intrusion. Then he recognized her.

"I'm crying too." Sarah Lander said, "They were my good friends." Her voice was more gentle than he'd ever heard it.

"You said something one night back in the Valley," said Eric slowly. "You said the good guys get shot at first. I guess you were right."

"Yes. But I also said, 'Don't let that stop you from being one of the good guys.' "

The longer they talked the softer their voices became. The shock, the anger, the sadness was mingled, tempered by their rethinking of the events they had so recently witnessed.

"I cannot ever, ever forget Dr. Ngambu," Eric said thoughtfully. "He showed me what it means to take responsibility for my own life. There's a lot more to it than looking out for Number One. It's looking out, the best I can, for everybody I touch."

"Now we *have* to get out of here," Sarah commented with deep feeling. "We must let the world know about Dr. Ngambu."

"And about David, too. He was as responsible in his place as the Doctor, but in a different way."

170

"True! There's another story to tell, too."

"Oh?"

"About Jakob Vroorman. In the end, he wouldn't let Ngambu outdo him."

"Yeah. There was something we all missed seeing in him."

Eric straightened and looked out over the camp. "You're so right, Sarah. We must get out of here. If only to let the world know there are people in it like those three."

They started walking toward the center of the camp.

"So, how do you think we can do it now?" asked Sarah.

"Just like David planned. An overland trek to Nairobi. I'm sure Lars will lead it. He was going to head the backup expedition if necessary, and I was to go with him. They've got to let me go along now."

"What about Alison?"

"She can take care of herself. She and I have been in a few tight spots together before."

Sarah stopped in the shadows and extended a hand.

"I'll help look out for her, just the same. And I just want you to know, Eric, I think you're one of the best of the good guys. I'll be praying for you on your trek."

Surprised at Sarah's relaxing of her toughness, Eric returned her grip warmly.

"Thanks, Sarah. You've been pretty great, yourself."

"OK. I think the Captain is looking for you. Get going before I start bawling again."

Eric moved away in the direction of the Captain and Lars and the plane crew. Mary was there, too.

"Lars has just been talking about plans for the expedition to Nairobi," the Captain said. "We think you ought to go if you'd care to volunteer."

"I just did," said Eric.

Mary Hastings held up the small, bleached monkey skull, which she had picked up after the Turnabo chief had thrown it down. "This was offered us in exchange for the Doctor and Jakob Vroorman. The Turnabos always pay their debts. It's a talisman that will see any of us safely through their country. Take it with you and show it to any natives you may encounter. They'll let you pass."

"We start in the morning?" asked Eric.

"Yes," said Lars. "After we bury David."

Alison agreed that Eric should go.

"You can do more good by going than staying here," she said. "There aren't enough people left for a second try, anyway. If you don't make it, we have no second chance."

"We'll make it. Here, the Captain and his people will handle the hunting. Mary will direct the nursing services. There will be plenty for you and Michelle and Sarah to do, helping her. Don't forget your journal. Who knows how important it will be later. Six or eight weeks of this will be rough, but you can make it, and we'll make it. OK?"

"Sure, it's OK, you big idiot." She clung to him tightly. "Oh, Eric—I can't forget that volcano. And I keep seeing those animals—and those natives—and—I'm afraid most of the time now, Eric."

"We all are, Sis."

The Mountain of the Sleeping Devil was utterly quiet

that night. Eric looked at it in the dawn light and thought of Dr. Ngambu and Jakob Vroorman. He forced himself to look away.

They buried David outside the camp, and, as soon as they could see their way through the tall grass and the jungle growth beyond, they set out. Lars, Eric, Mike Ainsworth, Joe Desmond, and Harry Maxwell. The good-byes were tearful.

Eric had become well acquainted with his companions for the trek. They had pulled their weight all the way. They had been on the firing line facing the baboons and the tribesmen.

Mike was happy-go-lucky, a rancher from the desolate outback of Australia. Joe and Harry were in the electronics business in Canada. They had played college football not too long ago.

The night before, they had studied Captain McGuire's navigation charts, which he had brought with him in his pilot's satchel. They had the charts now and a field compass plus their watches. Lars knew how to use these to navigate in open country.

Eric carried the monkey skull slung on a cord about his neck.

They followed the rim of the Valley for some time. Then they planned to turn east over the mountains where they hoped to intersect trails or roads leading south to Nairobi. Hopefully, in some of the villages they might find means of communication long before they reached Nairobi.

The route was not heavily overgrown. There was much savannah grassland with patches of acacia trees. Water was not difficult to find, although they went two or three days in the beginning before finding a small spring that flowed into the Valley. Hunting was good.

The first several days they made much better time than they had scheduled. Their greatest problem was navigation, and that was not difficult. Eric tried to keep his mind on his surroundings, and to not think of those who had died—or worry about Alison.

The rim of the Valley made a wide bulge to the west, away from the direction they wanted to go. They decided to cross the flat dry lands of the bulge, although they might have difficulty finding water. On the third day of their travel across the point they ran out.

They had now been gone from the camp for twenty-four days. They estimated another three or four days to finish the crossing and reach the distant foothills. Traveling late and starting early, they hoped to take advantage of every minute of daylight. On the next day the pangs of water starvation began to hit them.

"We're in trouble," said Lars as they halted on the second night since running out. "If we don't find water tomorrow, I suggest we try to go for it one at a time. If the first one out finds it he brings back a supply. If he doesn't make it, another one tries. There's bound to be some out there not too far away."

They agreed to the plan and bedded down for the night after making a meal of the last of the antelope meat they had shot yesterday.

The meat provided some liquid, but they could not go on for long without water. Eric tried to believe Lars was right. There had to be water in the foothills ahead.

The next day they made a noontime stop. "Tomorrow we'll make a one-man run for it," said Lars.

"Let's draw for who goes out first."

They drew. Eric got it and no one resisted. He was the youngest, and his anger was motivating him once more.

At daybreak, he left alone the next morning, marking carefully on a hand-drawn chart the location of his companions. He carried empty water canteens, his gun, and some dried meat.

He used all the tricks he had learned years ago in Scouts, and those Lars had taught him. He chewed grass. He kept a stone under his tongue. He padded fresh grass under the cloth he bound over his head.

Although he marched as rapidly as he could, the distant hills seemed to recede rather than come closer. He wondered now if separating from the group was the best thing to have done. It had to be. Each one of them mattered little now. But at least one had to get through if the main camp was to survive.

By noon he was forced to drop in the shade of an acacia. His dehydration made him dizzy, and his vision seemed to go out of focus and fade back in. He had delusions of sound. He thought for a time he was hearing Alison's voice urging him to get up and keep moving. Once he thought he heard the sound of an airplane passing close by. He drew a hand over his eyes and pressed his palms against his ears.

It was better to move, he thought. Resting only made his physical weakness worse. He got up and moved on, half staggering through the waist-high grass. His eyes squinted against the harsh sunlight. Overhead he saw the slow wheeling flight of a vulture.

But the sound didn't go away. The persistent sound

of an engine continued to throb in his brain. He shook his head and glanced up at the sky to assure himself there was nothing there.

He stared. He closed his eyes and pushed the heels of his hands into them. Then he looked again. His heart pounded hard.

A helicopter was cruising slowly only a couple of hundred feet above the grass a short distance to the east. It was no illusion. It was there!

But it was rapidly moving out of range. He fired a shot into the air, then another. He ripped off his shirt and waved it frantically.

The helicopter moved on.

Eric ran through the tall grass, waving and shouting. He fired his gun twice more. The image of the helicopter grew small in the distance. He collapsed in exhaustion, falling full length in the grass. His fist beat the earth in despair.

After a moment's rest, Eric began to think more clearly. What was the helicopter doing in a place like this anyway? Not to spot survivors, or they would have been scanning the ground.

"Of course!" he said, and he knew his answer had a ring of truth. "To survey the extent of the erupting volcano!" If he was right, there was a high probability they would circle the area again.

He looked for a clearing and set about deliberately to build a fire big enough to attract their attention. He had three precious matches. The dry chips burned strongly, but the boughs necessary for a big enough flame resisted them and the fire died before his eyes.

No sign of the helicopter yet.

He thought of setting a match to the tall grass, but he feared he would either be suffocated by the smoke or hidden by it. He gathered more dry grass and chips. Once more the effort was a failure.

When he heard the engine again and saw the helicopter hovering in his general direction, Eric made one of the most difficult decisions of his life. He reached for Dr. Ngambu's packet, tore the sheets out, and crumpled them into little nuggets.

The combination of paper, wood, and dry grass did the trick. The fire flared skyward just in time. The helicopter changed its course in his direction. Soon he saw faces in the chopper's windows.

Eric collapsed in exhaustion and relief.

"Thank God! Thank God! Thank God!"

These were the only words punctuating Eric's sobs when they found him.

When he remembered Dr. Ngambu's documents, he became inconsolable. He wept for his broken promise. For all the senseless deaths. But most of all for Dr. Ngambu—President Ngambu—that gallant man who had given more than his life. Some of the most important history of his new government had perished with him.

They led him gently to the small chopper.

They introduced themselves as Captain Roderick of the Kenya Resources Department and two scientists whose names Eric quickly forgot. They were indeed on their way to photograph the Sleeping Devil volcano.

There was disbelief in the faces of his listeners as he tried to describe the fate of the 747. If they hadn't heard about its mysterious disappearance earlier in the month, he knew they would have thought him mad.

"If you will direct me," Captain Roderick said finally, "we will take you back to your scouting team and then to the camp on the escarpment."

When they were airborne the Captain reached for the radio to pass the unbelievable story to Nairobi control.

Eric knew he had to stop him.

"Please don't notify Nairobi that you have found us! We were shot down on a direct course for Nairobi. A normal search would have taken place along that route and we should have been found the next day at least."

The look in their faces convinced Eric he had to control his voice.

"Our Captain is certain that the searchers were deliberately sent astray by someone in aircraft communications and control who were working with the terrorists.

"If that person—or persons—learn we have been found, they will run for it before they can be caught!"

The Captain frowned.

"That's a pretty serious conclusion you've reached. It would be almost impossible to carry out—"

"Will you wait at least until you talk to Captain McGuire?"

"Of course." Roderick could see that the strain was becoming too much for his passenger. "You say you have twenty or more stretcher cases back at your main camp, and over a hundred and twenty able people?"

"That's correct, Sir." Eric answered. "We have lost many since the crash."

"There is only one plane available to handle the

rescue operation. Fortunately, it's at Nairobi.

"The volcanic expedition has a base about ten miles from here. Two more small helicopters are based there. We'll drop our scientists at the base, then take the rest of you back to your camp. From there we can take your Captain and one or two others to Nairobi to report the situation. They can alert the authorities about the possible criminal action in airport control.

"We'll quietly alert the hospitals; then get the big plane to bring your people in. Is that satisfactory?"

Eric breathed deeply in relief.

"That sounds great."

The two scientists were dropped at their base and immediately took off in another ship to resume their work. Then Captain Roderick took Eric back to pick up Lars and the rest of the scouting party. From there, they flew to the main camp.

The helicopter landed on the grassy plain where the Turnabos had so recently made their savage camp. The people ran toward it in unbelieving hysteria, crying and laughing at the incredible sight of the rescue ship. They patted the surface of the helicopter and ran their hands over it lovingly. When Captain Roderick appeared, they flung their arms about him and kissed him.

Captain McGuire came through the crowd and extended a hand to Captain Roderick.

"I'm Captain McGuire of Flight 106. We're mighty glad to see you."

Eric and his companions climbed from the copter as the two men conversed. Eric's request that news of their finding be kept secret was confirmed. "I'm glad Eric thought to ask that of you," McGuire responded.

"Now, who's coming back with us on the first flight?" asked Captain Roderick. "We'll have to stop at the base to refuel, and we can only take a couple all the way to Nairobi. Do you want to go with us?"

"I'll stay until all the rest are out. I'll send my co-pilot, Mr. Thomas, to represent me, and I'll send the young fellow you picked up, Eric Thorne. His father will probably be at Nairobi. Dr. Thorne can handle official notification of the rescue to the press and he can also handle any personal messages some of these people might want to send home. Eric can take those with him. How about it, Eric?"

"May I talk to you privately for a moment?" was Eric's response. He gave Alison a wild bear hug as he and the Captain moved away from the jubilant scene.

"I didn't want to refuse your order in front of everybody, Captain McGuire, but I hope you will reconsider it," Eric began.

"After all we've been through together I just couldn't leave Alison behind. She wouldn't object, maybe, but I'm sure she wouldn't go out ahead of me. Setting down at Nairobi will be one of the greatest moments of our lives. I think we should share it."

Eric knew he had not disappointed the Captain by the look in his Irish eyes.

"I may have too many ideas for my own good, Sir, but I have a suggestion for a replacement."

Captain McGuire nodded for him to go on.

"It's Sarah Lander, Captain. Not only because she has been a real brick during these nightmares, but I think she deserves the chance to file her story first after all she has been through. She could also brief the press

181

for our arrival."

Captain McGuire reached for Eric's hand and shook it warmly. It was obvious he couldn't speak. This man who had resisted any display of emotion for so long was indulging himself a little in response to this young man he had grown to love.

"Sarah Lander will go in place of Eric Thorne," he announced seconds later. "She will send the good news of your safety to one relative or friend."

Notes were hastily written on sheets from the helicopter's captain's log pads and handed to a wildly happy Sarah.

"I hope it's a long time before I tackle another story that's this hard to get," she commented. "On second thought, I only wish I were a better writer to tell the story of Dr. Ngambu and Jakob Vroorman walking out to face those savages!"

"Is anybody good enough to do that?" Lars asked.

Sarah sought out Eric before she left to thank him for suggesting her name to Captain McGuire.

"You don't miss a thing, do you?" Eric teased. "As a matter of fact, if you think you owe me one, there is one question Alison and I have been itching to ask you."

"OK. Shoot."

"Did the State Department ask you to keep an eye on us on this trip?"

"Sorry kids, you'll have to buy some itching powder. That's one question I'll have to let go unanswered."

As she hurried off, she turned and gave them a knowing wink. Both Eric and Alison felt they had their answer.

Epilogue

It was an hour past sunset on the following day when the helicopter containing the final survivors approached Nairobi. Its passengers watched as the lights of the city gleamed on the horizon quite suddenly and seemed slowly to draw near.

"Just look at us!" Alison said with a sudden rush of consciousness about her appearance. "And there will probably be photographers!"

They were a strange looking group indeed.

Captain McGuire's only remaining badge of authority was his battered cap. Eric was wearing one of Lars' safari jackets with shoulders that drooped down his arms. The long tanned legs beneath his shorts were a welter of insect bites, cuts, and bruises. He was wearing dress shocs!

Alison looked at her long black hair now braided and tied with strips of rag, its luster long dulled by desert sweat and falling ash. She had put together an outfit from the only clean clothes they could find—all impossibly warm for desert wear. She completed the outfit with a pair of summer evening sandals Sarah had been carrying in one of her camera bags.

Michelle and Laurence were wearing the same clothes they had worn when the airliner crashed. They had a dingy, crumpled look in spite of Michelle's successive washings in their ration of water.

Michelle was carrying a pink stuffed toy.

The best dressed survivor award went to Mary Hastings. She looked almost normal in a clean safari blouse that all but eclipsed a tattered skirt. When asked where she had kept it hidden all this time, she answered in a borrowed accent she often reverted to for humor.

"Let's just say I was a-savin' it for me burial!"

She meant to be funny, but the impact of her words was disastrous. There was an awkward silence and more than a few tears were quickly wiped away.

Then came laughter. Raucous, almost hysterical belly laughter, but still close to tears. The remark was like a cypher key that removed the terrible total—or started to. They hugged each other and promised always to keep in touch.

The large helicopter had come to its destination in a corner of the airport where a row of ambulances waited, their red, unnerving lights circulating in the twilight. Eric looked out and saw a United States Air Force plane. It looked almost as good as the first helicopter the previous day.

Suddenly faces came into focus. A cluster of Red Cross people. Security officers. And a bevy of press men and women with cameras, as Alison had feared.

First out of the cabin, Eric and Alison were blinded by a burst of flashbulbs. It was the photograph sent by satellite to a hungry media in Europe and the United States.

Together they rushed down the steps and together into a pair of strong arms, unmistakably their father's. They knew their flight of terror was over at last.

Dr. Thorne held them at arm's length, letting his eyes caress them eagerly.

"Alison, Eric—" His voice choked with emotion as he said the words over and over. "Are you really here? Thank God! You made it! And Gramps—"

"Is Gramps here?" the twins asked, in unison.

"No, but the President ordered a plane for you and the other U.S. survivors. I know Gramps would have come himself if you had been among the injured. Sarah Lander assured us you weren't. She said a good many other things about you that made me *very* proud!"

Eric and Alison were able to convince the hospital team they were all right and should be released to go with their father. He assured them they'd meet their fellow survivors at a press conference in the morning. Dr. Thorne then led them to a waiting car.

He didn't herd them as he might have done a month earlier out of long habit. The difference was marked but unexpressed. In that moment, at least, his sixteen-year-old son and daughter seemed like adults to their father. They had fought for their lives and the lives of others in the Valley of Death, the world's most inhospitable desert.

There was a new maturity, a fresh nobility about them.

"If you only knew—if you only knew!" he kept repeating as the car moved away from the airport glare and headed for the city. He held their hands tightly.

They knew. Much better than he could have told them. There were new deep-grooved worry lines on his dear face. His hair was grayer than they had remembered it. He, too, seemed to have aged.

At the hotel the twins luxuriated in the hot showers and the late supper he had ordered. Except for the food brought by the first rescue helicopter, this was the first "civilized" meal they had seen since their departure from London five weeks earlier.

They sat and talked into the night. About the attack plane. The heat. The crash. Their desperate climb to the plateau. The volcano. The attacks by fear-crazed baboons. And at last, with great difficulty, of David Bjornson, Jakob Vroorman, Dr. Ngambu, and the Turnabo tribesmen.

Dr. Thorne listened. When the verbal tide finally was spent, there were tears in his eyes.

"What a tragedy—a man like Ngambu. I heard his name a few times when I was in London. I'd heard rumors about his election to the presidency of his country. What an honor it was for you to have known him!"

"He tried to save everyone," Eric said reverently. "He took each one who died as his personal responsibility—even his enemies."

"He saved us twice—when you come to think of it," Alison added. "I think he would be proud to know it was his burning documents that fed the signal fire which the rescue plane saw, just in time."

"I feel I owe him something for that," Eric said with emotion.

Just then Alison remembered the case that held their father's research which she had guarded now for so many days. Dr. Thorne was overwhelmed.

"Do you mean to tell me the two of you carried this through it all? And brought it back for me?"

"What else, dear Daddy?" Alison crooned, combing her freshly washed hair. "Isn't the family motto 'Dig in and pull harder'?"

The next morning the phone began to ring at dawn. Gramps in Washington. Aunt Rose at Ivy. Requests for magazine and TV interviews. These were referred to Mary, Gramps' executive secretary.

As they were leaving for the press conference the following morning, Dr. Thorne received news that two air controllers at the Nairobi airport had been arrested. They had boastfully confessed their part collaborating with terrorists and misdirecting the search for the airliner carrying President-elect Ngambu.

In the evening Dr. Thorne hosted a dinner—a Thanks-to-God celebration, he called it—for all the survivors who could come.

Mary Hastings had flight plans to return to her jungle outpost after a week's stay in Nairobi.

Sarah Lander was off for London within hours after the dinner to write the top story of her career. She would tell some, of course, in her syndicated column. But most of the story she would save to put in a book. She left still burdened by misgivings as to whether she could do justice to the heroism of the previous weeks' experiences.

Michelle and Laurence went on to South Africa, intent upon the possibilities of a new life there.

A few resumed their interrupted journeys.

Eric and Alison decided to pick up where they had left off, so they did not fly home on the Air Force jet, as did most of the North American survivors.

Before the company went their way, Dr. Thorne stood before them. "I must agree with Sarah Lander," he said with deep feeling.

"In this world the good guys get shot at first. But, don't let that stop you from being one of the good guys! We salute the memory of some of the world's best among the good guys—Alfred Ngambu, David Bjornson, Jakob Vroorman!"

Eric and Alison saw them all off the next day. Their father still had time to make his important conference for the International Agricultural Foundation in Capetown. Michelle cried, and Dr. Thorne patted his briefcase as he paused to wave at the door of his plane. They understood his grateful gesture.

The twins would follow on a later flight. They had been asked to take part in a debriefing session for the airline by Captain McGuire. Alison's journal entries would prove to be valuable after all.

Finally they were free to board their own flight to Capetown and to rejoin their father.

There were moments of uneasiness as the plane waited for a signal from the tower. A bit of anxiousness when they felt the tug of the jet's engines in takeoff and heard the landing gear retract.

"Want to put it all behind you for a while and play The Game?" Alison teased when the ship had found its altitude and the 'Fasten Your Seat Belts' sign was turned off.

Eric gave her one of those looks that could be interpreted as meaning, "Silly girl. That's one more thing we have outgrown!"

Alison clearly understood that look. "Speak for yourself, Eric," she shot back with a wink. "*You* may have outgrown The Game of making up stories about people we see. I'll never give up playing it!"

"Never in our wildest imagination could we have invented a Dr. Ngambu. Or come up with a character like Jakob Vroorman. Or a Mary Hastings. Even a Sarah Lander," Eric added thoughtfully.

"C'mon, then, and play The Game with me, Eric. It might be easier now to imagine the kinds of people God has around us, here in *this* plane."

Eric shook his head.

"I'm not in a mood for that yet. And I don't want to dull the memory of all those unforgettable people. Even Sarah—as good a writer as she is—will never really be able to tell the whole story. God alone can put all the pieces together."

Alison turned toward the window to watch the last pink clouds turn to soft grey embers. Beside her, out of the corner of his eye, Eric was watching the young couple across the aisle.

He touched Alison's hand to get her attention.

From the side of his mouth he whispered, "Hey, notice the newlyweds. Just married. On their honeymoon. Get a load of the tennis racquets and camera cases under their seats."

Alison smiled. "Here we go," she murmured.

"Excuse me—" Eric's thoughts were broken some seconds later when a crisp baritone voice filtered across the aisle.

"My sister and I could not help recognizing you from all the pictures we have seen in the papers recently. You *are* Eric and Alison Thorne?"

Eric turned toward the speaker. He seemed pleasant enough. His sister? Well, she was quite interesting. Her golden hair, cut close to her head, gave her fine features an elfin quality. He felt her very blue eyes gently searching his face.

Alison leaned forward with interested response to the speaker.

"Yes, we're Eric and Alison," she said with an almost too quick readiness to become involved in the conversation.

"We are Bryan and June Jeffery," he said warmly, extending his hand to Eric. "My sister and I have been on holiday in London and are returning to Capetown. Our parents have a ranch about twenty miles from the city. Will you be in the area long enough to be our guests for a weekend, say?"

Alison smiled and nodded positively for them both. She would have been blind to miss the interest in Bryan's eyes.

"Hey, slow down, Sis," Eric said by a look in her direction.

"Well, that might be very interesting. Thank you," Eric responded to the invitation with steadied deliberation.

"Here, I'll draw you a sketch to show how to get there and all that."

When map and telephone numbers had been exchanged a few moments later, Eric was glad the new acquaintances did not pursue the conversation. He liked that about them. They seemed to sense that he was not ready for small talk.

He still had some thinking to do about the events of recent days. Alison was in a similar mood.

Gradually they began to talk quietly together about the things they would probably never tell anyone else. Finally Alison asked:

"Remember what Mary Hastings said just before we crashed?" She went on without waiting for his answer.

"She said, It's up to God now, and whatever He allows will be all right."

Eric looked thoughtful. "Mmmm—I can see some of the good. None of us could watch those two men give up their lives for us and then go on being the same kinds of persons as before," he answered.

"You're right."

"It's made me realize that my life has value when I accept the responsibility for helping others. Who knows—I might even become a doctor," Eric mused.

"Hey, you are doing some thinking! I'm not ready to think that hard about the future. Not yet, anyway.

"But I'm alive!" she continued. "I'm ready to live in 'God's today,' as Mary Hastings called it. 'Doing whatever is good, wherever I can, one moment at a time, God helping me.' "

There was a moment of silence between them.

"Hey there, Twinny. More of Mary Hastings rubbed off on you than I realized. I guess we've both got a lot to think about."

The *Thorne Twins* Adventure Books
by Dayle Courtney

#1—*Flight to Terror*
Eric and Alison's airliner is shot down by terrorists over the African desert (*2713*).

#2—*Escape From Eden*
Shipwrecked on the island of Molokai in Hawaii, Eric must escape from the Children of Eden, a colony formed by a religious cult (*2712*).

#3—*The Knife With Eyes*
Alison searches for a priceless lost art form on the Isle of Skye in Scotland (*2716*).

#4—*The Ivy Plot*
Eric and Alison infiltrate a Nazi organization in their hometown of Ivy, Illinois (*2714*).

#5—*Operation Doomsday*
Lost while skiing in the Colorado Rockies, the twins uncover a plot against the U.S. nuclear defense system (*2711*).

#6—*Omen of the Flying Light*
Staying at a ghost town in New Mexico, Eric and Alison discover a UFO and the forces that operate it (*2715*).

Available at your Christian bookstore or from Standard Publishing.